EGGNOG, MISTLETOE, & NOAH ST. JAMES

J. S. COOPER

Blurb

Noah St. James is the grump who stole Christmas.

Seriously...Christmas used to be my favorite time of year. The presents, the spiked eggnog, kissing handsome men under the mistletoe. Then he came into my life. Or, rather, I came into his life under a bit of a pretense.

It's not my fault I wanted to surprise my boyfriend on the train home to visit his parents. How could I have foreseen that he would dump me, and then I'd have to pretend I was on the train for another reason? Surely, I couldn't have known fate would play a helping hand by having a driver at the station holding up a placard and thinking I was the said recipient. And yes, I did lie slightly when I said I was the Annie they were waiting for. But I was going to tell them the truth after I slid into the limo. I just needed my boyfriend to see I didn't care he was a two-timing weasel. I didn't know I was going to meet Noah St. James in the back seat. And after his snarky comment about me being late, I knew I wanted to bring him down a peg or two.

It had nothing to do with his turquoise-blue eyes. Or the fact that he made movie stars look ugly. Or the way my heart raced when I caught him staring at my lips. So yes, I pretended to be the nanny the St. James family had hired to look after Noah's sister's three young kids for Christmas. It was only going to be for a month. Besides, I needed a job anyway. And the house and family were Hallmark perfect.

I didn't account for the fact that I'm not good with kids, and I can't clean very well. And Noah St. James seems to be on to me. Why else would he be popping up everywhere I go? I just keep telling myself that I only need to last thirty days. And maybe, just maybe this will be the best Christmas of my life.

Prologue

Noah St. James is not what happy Christmases are made of. He's the scrooge of the season, and of course, he's my new boss. Kinda sort of. He's the man who signs my paycheck. Though technically, I don't work for him. And if we're being even more technical, this isn't even supposed to be my job. My friends would laugh out loud if they knew I was a nanny for the Christmas season. Anyone who knows me knows I'm not good with children. I mean, I'm not "leave them in a hot car" or "hit them with a frying pan" bad. But I'm never going to be called the next Mary Poppins or Mrs. Doubtfire. And the kids, they're not even Noah's. They belong to his younger sister, Lulu. But he's the one who runs the family business, so he's in charge of all the expenses for their month-long Christmas celebration.

I suppose you're wondering how I, Taytum Ana Cromwell, fashionista-in-training, became the nanny to three precocious and naughty as Hades children? Well, that's a story you don't want to miss. In fact, staring into the aquamarine eyes of Noah St. James almost makes up for the fact that I have the job from hell. Almost...

Chapter 1

I ADMIT IT. I WATCH TOO MANY HALLMARK MOVIES. I mean, is that really a crime? Did I think that the emotional sap provided by watching the same five actors fall in love with the same eight actresses would ruin my life? Certainly not. If I had thought that, then I wouldn't have packed a suitcase and rushed to the train station to surprise my boyfriend of two months on a trip to meet his parents for Christmas. Maybe I should have asked him if he wanted me to join him. Maybe I shouldn't have assumed that it would be a super-romantic gesture that would result in us getting engaged or at least becoming Facebook official. To be honest, it wasn't even my idea. We can blame my best friend, Danielle Emery Goldhawk, for that. Not only has she been watching too many Hall-mark movies but she's been reading too many romance books as well. In her head, we're both just a hot one-night stand away from getting knocked up by the billionaire asshole of our dreams. Not that we've ever met a billionaire, for that matter. Or, if I'm being more specific, an alpha billionaire who wants to have his wicked way with us and makes us orgasm all day and night. We don't run in those circles.

So anyway, I'm sure you're already cringing for me. Picture the scene. It's seven thirty on a Friday night. The train is about to leave Penn Station in New York City and make its way to Little Kimble, Connecticut. A small town right next to Greenwich. Only it's even richer than Greenwich. I looked online, and the median income is $345,000. Yes, you read that right. I barely make $45,000 a year, so that's a lot to me. But it's normal for the rich spawn who live in Little Kimble. That's where my boyfriend, um, ex-boyfriend now, grew up. Donovan Elias Jefferson Adams is his name. I should have known he'd be a douche by his pretentious name, but I kinda sorta was too busy paying attention to his vibrant blue eyes to pay attention to his moniker. Donovan is the sort of guy you meet that you know comes from money. He dresses in that preppy country club way that's totally douchey but still kinda hot. With his Sperrys, Ralph Lauren shirts, and khaki slacks, he has that self-assured smile that hot guys always have. And that cocky grin that comes from money. Really, he had it all—looks, money, a great job...I should have known it was too good to be true. We met at a bar, then went on a couple of dates. Had some bad sex he said was due to stress at work, though I wondered why he couldn't please me with his tongue or something. I mean, anything just to get me off, right? But still, I had hope. I wanted to live my *Sex in the City* dream. That's why I moved to New York in the first place. I knew I would never make the big bucks as an illustrator for children's books, but I figured I could have an epic love life. I figured wrong.

I know, I know, I should continue. I've digressed long enough. There I was, running in my Adidas sneakers because I didn't have money for Jimmy Choos or a cab and because the train was late (the MTA never cares about getting me anywhere on time). So there I am, running in my all-white, slightly too-tight Adidas because I got them at an outlet factory, and they didn't have my size. Alright, they had my size, but I bought one size too small because I didn't want to look like BigFoot. And well, I was paying for my vanity because I could feel the blisters forming as I ran. So there I was, running to the train with my ticket, feeling like I was in a movie with invisible cameras following me. I could almost picture the moment Donovan saw me and swept me up into his arms. Yeah, I really was delusional.

———

"*I*'m thinking that I'm going to change my name to Electra." Danielle giggled into the phone as I made my way through Penn Station.

"Electra?" I frowned, her words making me pause as I ran through the station. "Why Electra?" I asked with bated breath. Danielle was always coming up with new monikers to represent herself.

"I don't know. I think it just sounds really cool, don't you?" She paused as if waiting for me to agree. When I didn't, she exclaimed dramatically, "Hello, I'm Electra...doesn't that make me sound cool, like some sort of badass rock star?"

"Um, no. It makes me think of Carmen Electra, and she's stunning and almost a pinup girl. Do you really want guys to picture her when you tell them your name? Do you want them to ask you for topless pics within minutes of meeting you?" So I knew I was being fairly dramatic, but the situation called for it. Electra was just not the name a woman chose for herself if she wanted to be taken seriously.

"No." She sighed. "I mean, maybe actually, what's so wrong with them thinking about Carmen

Electra when they look at me?" She giggled. "Just means I'm hot."

"Because they're going to expect you to be some sort of sex bomb."

"Are you saying I'm not a sex bomb, Taytum?"

"I'm not saying that," I said quickly, not wanting to hurt her feelings. I paused as I tried to think of the right words to say. "But you don't want them thinking you're a porn star or something...trying to make money on that allyourfans site or whatever it's called."

"I'd love someone to pay me ten K for pics of my feet."

"Eww." I wrinkled my nose at the thought. "Hold on a second. I have to figure out what platform my train is leaving from. It would suck if I missed it."

"Okay," she said. "Also, you are too cool for school, my darling daring best friend." I couldn't tell if she was being sarcastic. It had been her idea for me to make a grand gesture, but a part of me thought that perhaps she'd been joking when she told me to surprise Donovan.

"You think so?" I asked, feeling slightly nervous. I was excited and hopeful, but I just couldn't shake the feeling that I was making a huge mistake.

"Uh, yeah. Donovan is going to be so excited to see you." She didn't sound positive, and that increased my anxiety tenfold.

"I hope so," I said. "I mean, it's not like he invited me to come, but I really feel like he was hinting and maybe hoping I would."

"Oh girl, he was definitely hinting something," she said, a wry tone in her voice. I could almost see her nodding even though we weren't on FaceTime.

"You think so, right?"

"Yeah. Didn't he say, 'Oh, it would've been so cool if you could come and spend Christmas with me and my family'?"

"Um, well, he didn't use those exact words," I admitted. "He said, 'I'm going home to spend Christmas with my family.' And I said, 'Oh, but I wanted us to spend Christmas together.' And he said, 'I know, that would've been really nice.' And I said, 'So why don't you skip?' And he said, 'I can't skip because I promised my parents I'd always come home for Christmas.'" I took a breath before I continued. "And then—"

"So you really don't like Electra?" Danielle interrupted me as if I weren't just sharing something really important with her. Granted, I'd already told her the story one or a hundred times before.

"Danielle, I was just telling you a story about—"

"I know." She sighed. "But why are your stories always so long?" I could hear her tapping her fingernails about something. "I know you like Donovan. I don't particularly care for him, but what I think doesn't matter. I encouraged you to surprise him because you need some answers, but do we have to constantly talk about—"

"Danielle, you have to listen to me. You're my best friend." It was my turn to interrupt her. "And it's not like you don't constantly talk about the same things all the time as well."

"I know." She giggled. "Continue then."

"Anyway, he finally said, 'Look, I'm not going to be able to spend Christmas with you.' And I said, 'Oh, it would be so nice to have met your parents.' And he said, 'I know my parents would absolutely love you.'" I paused. "So it wasn't an exact invitation, but why else would he say his parents—"

"It wasn't an invitation at all," Danielle said quickly, a curtness in her voice that reminded me that while she always encouraged me to do what I wanted, she didn't always think my reasons were the best.

"Well, I know it wasn't an invitation at all, but it was kind of like an invitation. I feel like maybe he was nervous to invite me because we've only been dating two months. And maybe he was scared that I'd think he was moving too quickly."

"Yeah," Danielle said doubtfully. "I mean, it is kind of quick, but—"

"I mean, when you know, you know, right?" I said, cutting her off. Danielle was silent on the other end. "Danielle, be honest with me. Do you think I'm making a mistake here?"

"Well, you know my point of view on this, Taytum. I think you should follow your heart. And if your heart is telling you to surprise Donovan on the train and go home with him, then that's what you should do."

"Yeah, my heart is telling me that this is my moment. I'm going to have my Hallmark Christmas movie magic this year. So that's what I'm going to do. I'm going to make it happen. I should see him in just over ten minutes," I said, feeling excited. "I'm going to get on the train, then I'm going to text him and be like, 'What carriage are you sitting in? I think I'm magic and can predict.'"

"Really?" she said, sounding doubtful about my plan.

"What?"

"That sounds hella goofy, Taytum."

"Well, it's obvious that I'm not magic. I just need to find out what carriage he's in so I can go sit with him."

"I know, but really? That's what you're going to say?"

"Danielle." I sighed. I didn't need her putting more doubts in my mind.

"It's Electra now." She sang into the phone as if she were Joan Jett.

I groaned. "Well, Electra, it's time for me to go."

"Okay," she said quickly. "And good luck."

"Good luck. I love you."

"Call me as soon as you get there. Okay?" She sounded worried.

"I will."

"And if you need me to—"

"It will be fine." I cut her off, knowing what she was about to say.

"Okay, fine."

We hung up, and I shook my head. I loved Danielle. We'd been best friends since we were five years old, but sometimes she was pretty self-absorbed. I knew she was trying to be a good best friend and support me, but I also knew she didn't think I was making the best decision ever, which I was still unsure of. I mean, in the movies, it always worked out. The guy was always happy or excited. Well, not in every movie, but in the best movies, that was how it worked out. And I really, really, really wanted a boyfriend for Christmas. My life was pretty much in shambles. I'd lost my job. My parents were going to the Caribbean for Christmas and said they didn't want any plus-ones. And well, my credit card bills were sky-high. I just needed some time to get away from my life and focus on the one good thing I had going. And that was Donovan's and my relationship. And yeah, maybe it wasn't the best relationship in the history of relationships, and maybe the sex wasn't the best sex I'd ever dreamed about. But he was handsome and fun and successful, and I could teach him how to go down on me better. Once we became more comfortable with each other.

I finally saw the time and platform number for my destination: Little Kimble, platform 7. I grabbed my bag and hurried. My heart was racing, and I was slightly nervous. I wasn't sure how Donovan would react. It wasn't every day you surprised your kind-of boyfriend on the train and said, 'I'm going to spend Christmas with you and your family because we should be moving our relationship to the next level.' He said he hoped to get married within the next five years and start a family. He was the one who told me that I was mommy material and had the most beautiful smile he'd ever seen. And yeah, he'd been drunk every single time, and it had been right before sex, but I believed him. A look in his eyes told me that he was absolutely in love with me. And yeah, we had never actually said I love you because who in New York City said I love you in a couple of months? No one. It wasn't like we were in Iowa or Nebraska or something.

In the city, things moved slower. However, I wanted Donovan to know that it didn't have to be as slow as molasses. I was into him and wanted a real relationship too. Shit, if he wanted to propose to me on New Year's Eve in front of his family, I'd be elated. Not that I was going to tell him that part unless I found a ring hidden in his closet and felt like he needed a little nudge. I smiled to myself as I got to platform 7.

I looked up and down to see if I could see Donovan. Maybe he'd be looking around for me, hoping I would surprise him on this train. Wouldn't that be something? What if we had something like ESP or something? What if he could read my mind, and I didn't even know?

I think you're the most handsome man in the world, Donovan, I thought. *If you can read my thoughts, please don't hate me for the other night when I wished you would last longer than five minutes. I know you were tired.*

I bit down on my lower lip. I was officially going crazy. I was talking to a man in my head hoping he could read my thoughts because if he could, that meant we were definitely soul mates. But seeing as I didn't hear any responses, I knew I didn't have ESP. And even more gratefully, I knew I wasn't crazy.

Chapter 2

THE TRAIN PULLED UP TO THE PLATFORM, AND I
hurriedly got on and looked for my seat. My heart
was racing, and I was excited. I loved catching trains.
I didn't know if it was because I had traveled
through Europe extensively while I was in college
and took trains everywhere, but something about
them was just so comforting to me. "Today, your life
is about to change," I whispered as I took my seat. I
looked up and saw a handsome man sitting in the
seat opposite me, and I beamed at him. He looked
like he was in his thirties, though he was dressed as if
he were an older college professor. He frowned back
at me, probably thinking I was some crazy chick
from the city. Maybe he thought I was a hippie, or
maybe he thought I was a supermodel. No, it was

obvious I was not a supermodel. I was not skinny enough or beautiful enough or fashionable enough, though it wasn't for lack of trying. I just didn't have the money. I mean, especially now that I had lost my latest contract for the Cool Today Publishing Company.

I was an illustrator of children's books. And while I didn't love children, I loved drawing, and I was very talented too. My artwork was featured in nineteen different children's books. One of the books had even won an award. I hadn't won an award, but it was still cool. I thought I was the luckiest person alive to be able to make a living from art. Something that my parents had told me my entire life would not be possible. And I was starting to think they were right, though, because Cool Today Publishing House had gone out of business. It turned out there wasn't a huge market for children's books targeting kids who thought they were animals. It had been cool illustrating the books, but even I had wondered how successful they would be in the market when I'd read the stories. I mean, one of the poems had said, "Today, I am a giraffe. I have a long neck, but I don't like it. So tomorrow, I will be a pig and *oink, oink, oink* my way to the farm. Then I'll become a cow and eat chocolate so I can make chocolate milk." I frowned as I thought about it. That had been a really shitty book. I didn't even know how the author had got a publishing deal. It hadn't surprised me when I found out they'd only sold twenty-two copies of the book.

It was sad. I mean, I was sadder for myself that they'd gone out of business and thus would not be hiring me to illustrate any more books. And I was starting to panic. I had some savings because Danielle, an accountant—even though she was crazy and wanted to change her name to Electra—had told me I should put ten percent of my paycheck into a rainy-day fund. I hadn't wanted to. I'd wanted to buy Birkin bags and Manolo Blahnik shoes, but ten percent of my salary wouldn't have afforded them anyway.

I was lucky that I'd listened to her because I'd been able to pay my rent this month. But I only had enough money left for two months' rent and minimum payments on my credit cards and a hundred dollars a month at the grocery store, which, who was I kidding, was what I'd normally spend in five days. But I could eat ramen. And now that I was going to spend Christmas with Donovan and his family, I'd save a shit ton of money. I wouldn't be using electricity. I wouldn't have to buy any food because his parents were rich. They would feed me, and they would not expect me to pay them back for anything like my parents would. The last time I'd gone to hang out with them, they told me I was eating them out of house and home and should contribute to the monthly grocery bill. Like, hello, Mom and Dad. You brought me into this world. You should be feeding me for free. But that's another story.

I realized I was mumbling under my breath, and the man sitting across from me was glancing at me with irritated looks. "Hey," I said quickly, "just want you to know I'm not crazy." He stared at me for a few seconds. "I mean, I know I was just mumbling under my breath because I was thinking about my parents and the last time I went to visit them in Florida and they told me I was eating them out of house and home just because I ate a couple of steaks and some salmon. Like, you're my parents. You brought me into this world when you had sex, you should have expected you were going to have to buy extra groceries. Am I right?" I stared at the man who just stared at me. I could see the disdain in his eyes, and I made a face. "Sorry. I'm not normally like this. I'm an illustrator and artist, and sometimes we're quirky, you know? I'm just nervous, and that's why I'm babbling. I'm going to surprise my boyfriend and his family for Christmas, and I think it's going to be amazing. I think he might even propose. Well, I don't really think he's going to propose. We've only been together for two months, but..." I bit down on my lower lip.

The incredibly rude man then pulled out AirPods from his pocket and placed them in his ears. "Well, sorry," I said under my breath. "Rude." I pulled out my phone and called my other best friend, Isabella.

"Hey girl, how's it going?" she said, answering the phone on the first ring.

"Um, I'm on the train sitting opposite this really rude guy," I said pointedly, glaring at him. He didn't even glance at me. I wondered if he was even listening to anything or if he was one of those nosy people paying attention to my phone call. "He's pretending that he's listening to music and he's not. He's totally listening to me talk about him."

"Um, are you okay, Taytum?" Isabella sounded confused, and I sighed.

"I'm just nervous. What if it doesn't go well? What if Donovan says that—"

"He'll be fine. Look, what's the worst that can happen?" she said.

"I don't know. Maybe he'll say he's not ready for me to meet his parents."

"Okay. Then you say, 'I'll come for a dinner, and afterward I'll go back to the city.'"

"True," I said. "I guess that's not so bad."

"It's not bad at all. Then at least you'll get to meet his parents. And best-case scenario," she said, "he's super excited, and he wants you to stay, and he was hoping you would come."

"True." Isabella was the reason I had decided to make this trip. She believed that every Hallmark movie was true. She was someone I'd met recently but loved.

"You're not really talking about someone on the train that's sitting on the seat in front of you, are you?"

"What do you mean?" I frowned.

"I mean, that would be so rude if you were doing that."

"Um, of course not. I was just pretending, of course, because I'm thinking about auditioning to be an actress and that was part of a script I was reading."

"Really?" Isabella said, and I rolled my eyes. Sometimes she was way too gullible. I loved that she was innocent and naïve and was basically there for me whenever I needed her, but the fact that she ate up whatever I said without even doubting it really made me question her sanity and her smarts. Danielle never believed my bullshit. It was a good thing she was super pretty. "Um, the train is leaving, Isabella, so I'm going to text Donovan now and see where he is. Wish me luck."

"Good luck, girl."

"Thank you." I bit down on my lower lip and

hung up. "This is it," I said to myself. The man in front of me rolled his eyes, and I decided to annoy him even more. "I've had the time of my life," I started singing loudly, feeling happy. Then I remembered there were other people on the train as well and pressed my lips shut.

Chapter 3

I TEXTED DONOVAN TWO TIMES AND WAITED FIVE minutes for him to respond, but he didn't answer either text. This wasn't going to work if he didn't respond. I bit down on my lower lip and thought for a second, working up my courage. Finally, I decided to call him. I thought the phone was about to go to voicemail when he eventually picked up. "Hey, what is it, Taytum? I'm on the train and headed home."

"I know," I said quickly. "I was just calling to wish you the most amazing trip home."

"Thanks, dude."

"Sorry, what?" I blinked. Had he called me dude?

"I said thank you. Um, is that all?"

"No," I said quickly. "I wanted to do a magic trick with you."

"Sorry, what?" He sounded irritated, which worried me.

"I think I have magical powers, and I want to—"

"Okay?" He cut me off, and I frowned.

"And I bet I can predict what carriage you're sitting in on your train."

"Okay, then. Go on."

"Well, no, you have to tell me."

"If I tell you, you'll just pretend that you got the number right." He was really getting on my nerves.

"Yeah, but..." I bit down on my lower lip. "Fine. Let me guess. You are in..." I paused as I noticed the man sitting across from me staring at me with an absolutely judgmental look on his face. I glared at him. "You're in carriage 8," I said, which I knew was incorrect because I was in carriage 8, and he certainly wasn't sitting here with me.

"Nope. I guess you don't have magical powers. Is that all, Taytum?"

"No," I said quickly, "you have to tell me what carriage you are in."

"Um, why?"

"Because maybe you really are in eight, and you just don't want me to know that I have magical powers because you are scared that I'll get fame and fortune and leave you and—"

"I'm in carriage 17, Taytum, and really I have to go. I don't like talking on the phone on the train."

"Oh, okay."

"It's just impolite to the other people."

"Sure. Okay. Bye."

"Goodbye." Then he hung up on me. He hung up as if my call wasn't something he'd been hoping for all evening.

I turned the phone off and put it into my handbag. I was feeling slightly deflated, and I didn't know why. He hadn't sounded excited to hear from me. He hadn't asked me what my plans were for the weekend. He didn't say he'd missed me. I just wasn't sure if he was one of those guys who didn't know how to show his feelings or if he was just getting fed up with me. What if he thought the sex was bad too? What if he blamed me, which would be absolutely ridiculous because he was the one coming, not me. I sighed. I looked at my suitcase for a few seconds, nervous that it might get stolen when I went to surprise Donovan. I took a deep breath and leaned forward to talk to the man across from me. "Please don't steal my case," I said. "I don't want to take it with me when I go to surprise my boyfriend, possible fiancé, because—"

"Ma'am, I have no interest in touching your case," the gentleman spoke, and my jaw dropped.

"So you do understand English?" I glared at him.

"Do you not understand that I'm not interested in having a conversation with you right now?"

"Huh? Whatever. I was trying to be polite because—"

"Ma'am, go and surprise your boyfriend or your fiancé or your future husband or whatever. Don't worry, I won't be touching your suitcase, and no, I'm not going to stop anyone else from touching it just in case that was going to be your next question."

"No need to be a jerk. It's the Christmas season, you know?" He rolled his eyes and unfolded the newspaper on his lap. "Well, anyway," I said as I sat up and made my way down the hallway to carriage 17. I was going to surprise Donovan, and I was super excited. I wondered if he'd burst into tears of happiness. That would be kind of cool. I mean, men didn't cry unless they were super emotional, so if he cried, that would mean it was really special to him. I took a deep breath as I got to carriage 17 and crossed my fingers for luck before I walked through the door. "Hey, Donovan, guess what?" I said, a tinge of hope, excitement, and all my dreams in my voice. My jaw dropped as my eyes took in the sight before me because there sat Donovan, but he wasn't alone. A cute little blonde was sitting on his lap and his hand was on her thigh rubbing back and forth, and he was kissing her neck and she was giggling. "What is going on here?" I exclaimed, like the dumbass that I was. Donovan's eyes widened as he stared at me and the girl looked at me curiously.

"Hi," she said. "Are you in this cabin as well?"

"No, I'm not. Donovan!"

He sighed. "What are you doing here, Taytum?"

"Oh, is that Taytum?" the girl said, looking me up and down. "Hi, I'm Alicia."

"What? Who are you?" I frowned. "You're not his sister, are you?" Which I knew was a stupid question to ask because would his sister be sitting on his lap and would he be nuzzling her? I mean, not if he wasn't some nasty incestuous creep, which I didn't think he was.

"Um, what are you doing here, Taytum?" Donovan said again.

"I was surprising you so I could go home and—"

"Um, what is she talking about?" the cute blonde said. "I'm sorry that Donovan broke your heart, but he's with me now."

"What?" My jaw dropped in shock at her comment.

"Um, I know that you don't like to face reality, but he dumped you, and he's with me, and—"

"You what?" I stared at Donovan.

"I tried to tell you, Taytum. It's over."

"It's over?"

"Yeah. I tried to tell you last week when I said, 'No, I'm not interested in going with you to get Greek food.'"

"You said you had to work late."

"Well, I didn't. You have to remember the next day when you asked me to get pizza, I also said no."

"You said you wanted to shop for a Christmas present for your mom."

"Yeah, he was with me," Alicia said. "He was buying me diamond earrings." She looked at him then. "I see what you mean...she's not in touch with reality." I stared at them both, and I took a deep breath. "You said what?" I bit down on my lower lip.

"I really hope you didn't catch this train to surprise me or think that something was going to happen," Donovan said slowly. He looked contrite, but I noticed that he wasn't that sorry for me because he wasn't moving that bitch off his lap.

"No, I didn't come on this train for you. I'm going to Little Kimble for another reason."

"Okay," he said. "Well, good luck."

"Thank you," I said. "I just wanted to say hello and meet this biatch." I started laughing. "Sorry. I hope you didn't think I meant bitch because I sure don't mean bitch. It's just the way us young folk call our friends, you know? Biatch. You're like a little biatch," I said again. She just blinked at me.

"Okay, well, you have a nice life," she said. And my jaw dropped again. That bitch really just told me to have a nice life?

"You too," I said, smiling widely. "Enjoy his little Pee Pee. Or maybe you call it Wee Wee or Little

Donovan. Don Don." I looked at Donovan. "And by the way, just in case you didn't know, I faked it every single time. You wouldn't know how to give an orgasm if you received instructions for dummies." I blinked back tears. I couldn't believe I'd wasted my time on this no-orgasm-giving loser. "Every single time." I reiterated before hurrying out of the carriage. I wasn't going to give him the opportunity to say anything or see the tears rolling down my cheeks. He wasn't worth a single tear, and I couldn't believe I'd ever convinced myself he was.

Chapter 4

I MADE MY WAY BACK TO MY CARRIAGE WITH MY TAIL between my legs. I didn't even want to look at the asshole sitting across from me. And I was glad he didn't look up from the newspaper when I sat down.

"Freaking Hallmark movies," I mumbled under my breath. I bit down on my lower lip to stop myself from crying.

"You're back quickly," the man said, and I looked up. I stared at him.

"Oh, so you're talking to me now?" I could hear the attitude in my voice, but I didn't care.

"I just made a comment. I wasn't talking to you," he said, his lips smirking at me. And I rolled my eyes and looked out of window.

"Do you know how long it is to Little Kimble?" I said, not looking at him as I asked the question. How long did I have to stay on this train before I could get another ticket to take me back to New York City? Which was the last thing I needed. What a waste of money.

"Shouldn't you know that if you got the ticket already?" he asked, and I turned to look at him again.

"Dude, what is your problem?"

"What's my problem?" He raised an eyebrow. "I take it that surprising the boyfriend didn't go well. I mean, soon-to-be fiancé." He chuckled slightly. "Though it's not looking like he's soon to be a husband in my book."

"And what's that supposed to mean?" I snapped.

"Well, I take it you found him on the train."

"Yes. And?"

"I take it he wasn't too happy you surprised him."

"Well, it's not my fault he's a lying scumbag douche."

"Oh boy," he said. "So what happened?"

"What do you mean what happened? When I was speaking to you earlier, you didn't want to even acknowledge I existed. You pulled out earphones and pretended that—"

"Well, now I'm invested."

"He has another girlfriend, okay? He's a dog. She thinks he broke up with me, but he totally didn't. He totally wanted me to come and surprise... Well, I mean, he didn't want me to come in any way whatsoever." I groaned. "But I know that's a bit of TMI."

"Um, I'll take your word for it," he said, smirking again.

"Whatever."

"And it's three hours."

"Three hours? I thought Connecticut was closer than that."

"Well, there are a number of stops, and one of the stops is slightly longer than normal." He shrugged. "You could have taken the fast train."

"I know I could have taken the fast train, but he wasn't going to be on the fast train. He… Oh, whatever. It doesn't matter." I sighed. "I'm going to play games on my phone, and I'm not going to turn the volume off. So you will have to listen to annoying music. And normally, if you were polite, I would make sure that the volume was off, but you're not polite, so I'm not going to bother turning the volume off. And—"

"Ma'am, you do you." I stared at him for a couple of seconds, and it was my turn to start laughing. He frowned slightly as he gazed at me.

"And just what is so funny?"

"You totally don't look like a guy who would say 'you do you.'"

"Really?" He shrugged. "And why is that?"

"Because you look so prim and proper and"—I shrug—"I don't know."

"It might be something that my little niece taught me." He smiled. "I don't know where she picked it up from because she's only five. But whenever her mom, who is my sister, asks her to do something, my little niece always says to her, 'You do you, Mommy.' And it doesn't even make sense in that context, but everyone in the family thinks it's funny."

"Sounds cute," I said with a smile. "So is that where you're off to then?"

"Sorry, what?"

"Is that who you're going to see in Little Kimble? Because I take it you don't live in Little Kimble. You just don't seem the sort of guy who would live in a small town."

"I don't." He nodded. "I'm actually going to meet my family for Christmas."

"Oh, yay. Another lucky guy is going to spend Christmas with his family."

He smiled. "Well, it's going to be a long time seeing as we spend thirty days together."

"Thirty days together? What?"

He nodded. "It's something my mom instituted. She loves the family to get together for long periods of time, so everyone is going to be there. My older brother, me, my two younger brothers, my younger sister, my niece and nephews, my parents." He shrugged. "Maybe some family friends."

"Oh, cool. And what about your and your brothers' wives?"

"None of us are married." He shook his head. "But I am a little bit lucky because I'm going to spend the first couple of days with a childhood friend before I go home."

"Oh, cool."

"Yeah. Her parents are planning a trip, and... Well, you don't need to know the details."

"No, I don't," I said curtly, which I knew was kind of rude and was a lie. I totally wanted to know every single detail of this man's life because I was just the sort of nosy person who wanted to know everything about everyone, no matter if I liked them or not. I was the sort of person who would scroll on Facebook and see that someone had liked one of my friends' posts, then click on their profile and check out their entire life and then click on their partner's profile and check out their entire life. After learning everything about them, I would then click on their parents' profiles and check out their lives, as well. There are hundreds, maybe thousands of people who existed in the world that I knew everything about and they didn't even know I existed. Sometimes I wanted to comment, "Not a good look, Bill," or "You're sounding like a desperado, Sally," but of course, I didn't. I wasn't that crazy.

"Well, I hope it all works out for you," he said, nodding his head.

"Yeah, thanks. I'm sure it will. I mean, I'm not going to get my picture-perfect Hallmark movie for Christmas, but hey, I guess that's why it's on TV and not in real life, right?" He pressed his lips together, and I could tell he was done with the conversation. He was so rude. And if I wasn't already heartbroken over what had happened, I would let him know again. But I just didn't have the energy, and I was actually grateful to him for making me angry so I wasn't crying. I heard my phone beeping, and I pulled it out. There was a text from Donovan.

Donovan: Hey, chica, sorry you had to find out about everything this way. I really do hope that you didn't catch this train for me.

I stared at his text. What a jackass. I responded to the text.

Me: Nope, didn't come for you. I was going to Little Kimble for another reason, thought I would say hello.

I pressed send. I hoped he didn't ask me what my other reason was because I had no idea what lie I could make up. I was about to call someone to tell them about what had happened when I realized that I still felt upset and the situation felt too raw. I was normally a happy-go-lucky person who looked at the bright side of life. But I wasn't sure I was ready to look at the bright side of this situation because there wasn't a bright side. How could there be a bright side? I thought I was on my way to getting engaged. I thought Donovan was going to tell me he loved me and be so thankful I had joined him. Instead, I got dumped. I had no job, no boyfriend, no money, no nothing. My life was going down the drain, and I didn't know what to do. Not only was I not having a Hallmark movie moment but it had turned into some sort of nightmare moment.

I racked my brain to think of a channel that showed a lot of horror movies, but I couldn't think of one because I didn't watch any. I let out a sigh. Maybe that was a sign I needed to change up my life. Maybe it was a sign I needed to get away from the sap and immaturity of hoping that everything would be like the movies because life just wasn't like that.

Chapter 5

THE TRAIN CONDUCTOR'S VOICE WAS LOUD AND melodic through the speaker. "Ladies and gentlemen, we are approaching Little Kimble. Please gather your bags. Once again, we are approaching the Little Kimble stop."

I bit down on my lower lip and looked out the window. It definitely looked picturesque outside. It reminded me of a quaint English village. Well, not that I'd seen one in person in a long time, but I watched a lot of murder-mystery shows set in England, my favorite being *Midsomer Murders*. And I just loved the English countryside.

"I think you should gather your bags." The guy sitting across from me spoke to me one last time.

"I did hear the speaker. I'm not the one with the earbuds in, thank you very much."

"I'm glad to hear that." He smiled and nodded. "Well, Merry Christmas to you, dear."

"Dear! You're acting like you're fifty years old and I'm fifteen." I frowned at him.

He chuckled slightly. "Well, maybe I said that because you've been acting like you're fifteen."

"And you act like you're seventy," I said, glaring at him.

He shrugged and stood. "Have a nice day."

"You too." I watched as he exited the carriage. When I was sure he was out of earshot, I mumbled under my breath, "Not."

I stretched slightly and gathered my suitcase. I wasn't quite sure how I was going to work this. It's not like I could get off the train, go to the counter, and ask for another ticket back to New York because God forbid Donovan and his bimbo saw me. I would be mortified. Absolutely mortified. What I would do is grab a taxi and head into town and get some dinner. After dinner, I'd return to the train station and head back to New York City. There was no way Donovan would see me then. And yeah, I didn't have the money to be catching umpteen taxis and buying food in a city I didn't know what the cost of living was going to be like. However, I had a credit card for situations like this. I was willing to go into a little bit of debt to save myself some embarrassment. Grabbing my suitcase, I headed out of the carriage as the train stopped. I stood by the doors, and as they opened, I stepped down. Looking around, I groaned when I saw Donovan and his bimbo headed toward me.

"Hey there," Donovan said, a smile on his face. I wanted to slap the smile off it.

"Hi," I said, trying not to glare at him. "Well, bye."

I walked ahead of them quickly. There was no way I was going to walk with them, not after everything that had gone down. We made our way through the doors into the small train station, and I looked around, feeling slightly nostalgic. I really was in small-town America, and I loved it. I headed out of the doors to the main street.

"By the way, Taytum." Donovan's voice sounded behind me, and I groaned.

I looked over my shoulder. "Yeah. Can I help you?"

"I just wanted to say that…"

I took a deep breath as he paused. I didn't want to hear what he had to say.

"Excuse me," a deep voice sounded from the road.

I looked up to see a chauffeur with an old-fashioned cap on his head, standing there with a sign.

The sign read, "Annie." I bit down on my lower lip and looked at him.

"Hi. Can I help you?"

"You looked slightly lost. You're not Annie, are you?"

I stared at him for a few seconds in confusion. I wanted to start singing "Tomorrow" from *Annie* but knew the man would wonder if I'd escaped from a mental institute. I was about to tell him he had the wrong person when I looked behind me again. There was Donovan and the bimbo coming up close to me.

"Yes, I am." The words were out of my mouth before I could stop them.

I turned around and looked at Donovan. "Sorry, my ride's here." I pointed at the limo behind the driver.

"You've got a limo picking you up?" Donovan looked shocked.

"Yeah. I told you I didn't get on the train for you. I got on the train because I had a special appointment in Little Kimble. We just happened to be on the same train. And I realized that, so I wanted to come and say hello."

"Annie, the family's waiting for you," the driver said, looking at me with a warm smile. His attention then moved to Donovan and the smile slipped from his face slightly. I liked this man already.

"The family?" Donovan frowned slightly. "What family?"

I licked my lips nervously. I had no idea what the driver was talking about.

"Annie here is our new Christmas nanny," the driver beamed.

"Yeah. I'm a Christmas nanny. Duh!" I stared at Donovan, and he frowned. "That's why I gave them my middle name of Annie," I said to him, "because when I'm with kids…" My brain searched furiously for words that would make sense. "I prefer them to call me Annie because it's hard for some kids to pronounce Taytum."

"I didn't know your middle name was Annie." Donovan cocked his head to the side. "I thought your middle name was.."

"Well, it is," I said. "Anyway"—I looked toward the driver—"I'm ready. Let's go. Bye," I said to Donovan.

The driver opened the back door for me. "In you go, ma'am."

"Thank you," I said with a smile. I slid into the back seat of the car and leaned back. I knew I couldn't keep the lie up. There was just no way possible. I'd wait until the driver drove a couple of blocks, then I'd tell him there'd been a mistake and I'd get out. I smiled to myself. "Take that, Donovan. Now, he can't possibly think I'd come for him."

"You're late," a deep voice said from next to me.

My whole body stilled as I turned to look at him. A tall man in a business suit with blue-green eyes stared at me. His lips were pressed together. He looked down at the very expensive-looking watch on his wrist. "I've been sitting here for thirty-five minutes waiting."

"Excuse me?" I stared at him, blinking.

"I said, 'You're late.'"

"The train just arrived. What did you want me to do about it?"

"I thought you were going to be on the earlier train. I thought ..."

"Well, I'm on this train, and I'm here now. So are we all good?"

I really hoped he wasn't going to be snappy and bitchy the entire couple of blocks I remained in the car. The driver got into the front seat and turned on the ignition.

"Mr. St. James, are we ready to go now?"

"Yes. Thank you, John," the man said with a slight nod. He turned to look at me as John raised the divider to give us privacy. I felt his eyes going up and down my body. "You're the nanny?"

"Yes, I am," I snapped at him. "Why couldn't I be a nanny?"

"Huh? And you have fifteen years of experience with children?"

I licked my lips nervously. Did I look like I had fifteen years of experience with children? I suppose I started babysitting when I was really young. "If I said I did, then I do," I said, glaring at him.

"Hmm," he said. "Well, my sister hired you. She knows what she's doing."

"Yes, she does. Thank you very much."

"I just hope you'll be worth a hundred grand."

"Sorry. What?" I stared at him in shock.

"Your pay for the month. A hundred grand."

"You're paying me a hundred grand for the month to be a nanny?" Please God, don't let me act too excited. Had I been living under a rock all this time? Was this now the going rate for holiday nannies? My jaw dropped. He had to be joking.

"Like dollars?" I asked him slowly.

"What other currency would I be paying you in?" he said, frowning slightly.

"Sorry, I must have misunderstood. I thought I was getting paid a different amount."

"Well, you said that you had offers from one of the royal families in Europe and from an A-list Hollywood star. And my sister really wanted you, and what my sister wants, my sister gets."

"A hundred grand for being a nanny for a month?"

"Yes," he said succinctly. "Why? Don't tell me

you want more money now? Did the president offer you a job too?"

"No," I said quickly, smiling at him. "Trust me, that will be fine."

Chapter 6

My brain was going a mile a minute.

A hundred grand! I wasn't a nanny, and I wasn't Annie, but this family didn't seem to know or care. Yeah, I didn't have much experience with kids, but how hard could it be? Kids were kids. I liked to play games. Some people thought I was a big kid myself. And a hundred grand for thirty days ... Shit, even I couldn't fuck that up.

I knew what I was thinking was absolutely crazy and maybe illegal, but could I pretend to be Annie? Could I do the job, make a hundred grand, and then go home without feeling guilty? It certainly would go a long way in fixing my broken heart. I looked over at the guy sitting next to me, Mr. St. James. I didn't even know his first name. I didn't even know his sister's name or the kids' names. But I learned pretty quickly. I was friendly and personable.

"So Annie. You said you have a degree in ... What was it exactly?"

I stared at the guy, wondering if he was trying to trick me. Did he already know what my degree was in and he was trying to figure out if I knew, or did he not know and was genuinely curious?

"Didn't you see my résumé?" I said lightly, trying to smile.

I wanted to have an attitude with him. He was getting on my nerves, but if he was my boss and signing my paycheck, I would be saccharine sweet.

"No, I didn't see your résumé, but I heard you had a whole heap of degrees."

"Oh, well, you know, I'm very modest. I don't like to talk about such things," I said quickly. "What was your first name again?"

He stared at me for a few seconds, and I couldn't help but notice how luscious his lips looked. It was then that I really paid attention to his appearance. The guy was absolutely gorgeous. Like drop-dead gorgeous. Like the most amazing-looking man I'd ever seen in my life. And I thought Donovan was hot, but compared to Donovan, this man was Adonis.

"Noah. I'm Noah. St. James."

"Oh yeah, I forgot," I said. "I was so focused on

trying to learn more about the kids and getting ready for the holiday season and making sure that they are really occupied." I frowned. That didn't sound like I knew much about kids. "I have a very modern and old-fashioned approach to child-rearing. I think kids should have a lot of fun but be educated at the same time. I think that ..."

"You're talking in circles, Annie." He frowned. "You think they should be educated while having fun, and you're old-fashioned and modern. I don't really see how you can be all of those things."

I stared at him for a few seconds, pressing my fingers together. "Don't go off on him, don't go off on him," I repeated under my breath. I'd had a long day and wasn't interested in talking with this man and bullshitting, but I'd do my best for a hundred grand. "Well, you know, different parents like different approaches. I ensure I'm best at all approaches so that I can deliver no matter what the parent wants."

"Okay, then. So you got into this career because you really love kids?"

"Yeah, I love them so much. When my ex asked what my favorite trip was, I always said Disney because there were so many cute kids." I paused. Did that make me sound like a creep? What single adult went to Disney to look at kids? Fuck. I didn't want him to think I was going to be some sort of psychopath or child kidnapper. That was the last thing I needed. I was Hallmark movies, not Lifetime. "I mean, Disney is fun for people of all ages. It just makes you feel like you're a big kid, you know?"

*N*oah frowned slightly and shrugged. "I wouldn't know. I've never been to Disney."

"Oh my gosh! Really? How have you never been to Disney? It's so much fun."

"It's not really my thing," he said, shaking his head, "but good to know you enjoy it. Maybe one night this week I can ask you some of the things you enjoy about it."

"Sure," I said. "Why, though?"

"Because we have a family-friendly hotel chain that we're opening in two years. We're in the planning stage right now, and I want to make sure that ..."

"You're building a hotel chain?" I stared at him in shock. "No way!"

He looked at me with a confused expression on his face. "I thought you spoke to my sister, and she told you about the family business."

I licked my lips nervously. Fuck! Of course, the real Annie would have spoken to his sister. No one got hired based on emails.

"Well, I really like to focus on the kids, and I'm not really into business, so I must not have paid much attention to that part."

"I see."

"So Annie…"

"Why don't you call me Taytum?" I said. "My name is Annie, of course, but I go by Taytum because my cousin was called Annie too. And my parents were really close with her parents, and it was just weird when they were both like, Annie, do this, Annie, don't do that. And my cousin Annie and I were always like, which one of us? And my parents were like the other Annie, and her parents were like the other Annie. And, well, suffice to say, they call me Taytum."

"You really do talk a lot, don't you?"

"Yeah."

"Hmm," he said. "Interesting."

"Oh, well, what's interesting about that? I find that ..."

"I'm sure it's related to your child-rearing tech-nique," he said, nodding. "And I'm sure that's why my sister hired you. She loves to talk as well."

"So it's going to be me, you, and your sister at the house, and her husband, or…?"

.   .   .

He stared at me and shook his head. "You really weren't paying attention, were you? I'm guessing as soon as you heard how much the pay was, you were excited to take the job without hearing any of the other facts."

"No, that's not why I took the job. I didn't even know it was going to be a hundred grand." I pressed my lips together. "So anyway, if you could just tell me who is going to be there so I can refresh my memory."

"Okay. Well, my parents will be there. Of course, the grandparents, it's Christmas." He frowned. "So my parents, me, my three brothers, my sister, her three kids."

"And her husband won't be there?"

He shook his head. "No. Unfortunately, her husband passed away."

· · ·

"Oh, I'm so sorry. I just didn't realize that. I ..."

"It's okay," he said, shaking his head. "It was definitely hard, but it's been a couple of years now, and she has us. And who knows, maybe one day she'll get married again."

"I couldn't imagine losing my husband," I said. "I'd be absolutely heartbroken. I would cry myself to sleep for years and months."

"Are you married?" he said.

"No. Why? Do I look married?" I looked down at my ring finger and wiggled my fingers. "I thought I was going to be getting married soon, but..." I paused.

. . .

*D*on't go down this route, I thought to myself, because if he asked you too many questions and you had to tell him the truth, or at least kind of the truth. Then it might come out that you're really Taytum, who was on the train to meet her boyfriend's parents for Christmas, and not Annie, who was on the train for this job and all this money.

"*A*nyway, what about you? Are you married?"

"*O*h no." He shook his head. "I don't ever foresee myself getting married."

*H*e paused and looked at my lips. "But I do see myself having a lot of fun."

Chapter 7

"So what does that mean exactly?" I said, staring at the man next to me.

*T*here was a smirk on his face, and for a couple of seconds, I could feel something tingling in my belly. I'd only felt that once before, and that was when I had been eighteen and went to a nightclub for the first time, and a really hot guy had come up to me and said, "You are absolutely stunning. I would fuck you right now if I could."

*O*f course, I just stared at him and walked away, but I'd been all aflutter. If I'd been more of a confident, outwardly sexy woman, then I would have been like, "Come on, let's do it." But I wasn't. I was the shy soul. And as much as I enjoyed sex and being hit on, I wanted it to feel more romantic than that.

"Do you really have to ask me what I mean?"

Noah looked me up and down, and I felt the butterflies in my stomach again.

*W*ell, you said you like to have fun, and I don't know what that means. Do you like to play board games? Do you like to play tennis? Are you really into chess?"

*D*o you really think that's what I'm talking about?" he asked, licking his lips and chuckling lightly. "Or do you think that ..."

I don't think anything," I said, looking away from him quickly. I was fast approaching dangerous territory. "I'm just here for a job."

.   .   .

"You're not here to snag a rich St. James brother?"

I stared at him for a couple of seconds. "I didn't even know you were rich." Which was true. I didn't know if he was rich. I'd never even heard of him up until thirty minutes ago.

"You didn't think that a family that was going to pay you a hundred grand for one month of nannying was rich?" He nodded. "You're not even blond."

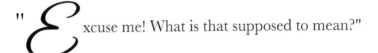

"Excuse me! What is that supposed to mean?"

"What do you think it means?"

"I take offense to that. I have many blond friends who are not dumb."

· · ·

"So then you admit you knew what I was saying?"

"Yeah, but that was rude. That was ..."

"Oh no, no. Don't tell me you're another woke millennial." He started chuckling then.

"That is so rude. I don't like the term millennial, and I don't like the term woke, either."

"Oh, but Annie, I really think there will be many things in life you don't like, and you're just going to have to deal with them. I'd be more than happy to teach you to grow a backbone."

"I don't need you to teach me to grow a backbone. Thank you very much." He put his hand on my knee, and I thought I was going to faint.

"*T*here are other things I can teach you as well."

*M*y eyes widened, and I stared at his fingers. "What are you doing?"

"*F*lirting with you. Or do you millennials don't know what it means to flirt? I suppose all you know is a winky face and a text message."

"*Y*ou're not even that much older than me. Thank you very much. Don't tell me you've never sent an emoticon in a text message."

"*I* do not send emoticons or emojis." He shook his head. "I very rarely send texts as well. If I have something to say, I'm short and succinct. And that is much easier over the phone or in person."

"Oh my gosh! So you don't send texts, whoop-de-doo. I guess you don't have any friends, either."

"I have friends, but we hang out in real life."

"And what about the women you date?"

"Oh, so you're curious whether I'm in a relationship, are you?"

"No, I'm not curious if you're in a relationship," I said quickly. "Why would I care if you were in a relationship? Why would you think that?"

· · ·

"**W**hy did you even bring it up? And why does thou protesteth so much?"

"**T**hou does not protesteth so much," I said quickly before frowning. "Wait, does that make sense? I mean, me does not protesteth so much, or I'm not protesting, whatever," I said, glaring at him.

"**I** know what you said." He smiled. "You came for a job. You want to make a hundred K. Get in, get out. That's your motto, right?"

I bit down on my lower lip. "You really don't have a good impression of me, do you?"

"Well, my sister told me that you were asking all about my brothers and me. So which one of us do you have your eyes set on?"

I blinked at him. "I was only trying to figure out the family dynamics because that makes a difference when you're rearing children."

"But you're not rearing children, dear. You're a part-time nanny for the Christmas season. The kids will be with their mother for much of the time. And my parents, their grandparents, dote upon them. You'll have plenty of free time."

"Yeah, well, that's good," I said. I cleared my throat. Maybe this wasn't a good idea. Yeah, I needed the money, and a hundred grand would go a long, long way. Perhaps I could even write my own children's book and illustrate it and try to sell it to a publisher. And that would be really cool. But I didn't know if I would be able to put up with Noah St. James. And it wasn't just the fact that he was an asshole and rude and asinine. It was the fact that he was also gorgeous and sexy and made me feel things I thought only happened in X-rated movies. I didn't need the temptation. I was taking this job to look after kids. I didn't need to fall into the uncle's bed. Because I was pretty confident that was what Noah was offering. He, if the way he squeezed my knee was to be believed, was interested in having some fun-fun with me. And I knew I wasn't strong enough to keep saying no. If he snuck into my room one night in his boxers looking all sexy, his blue eyes looking me up and down, and his pink tongue licking those luscious lips, I had a feeling I would invite him into my bed. I had a feeling that my panties and bra would be off faster than I could blink, and I wouldn't feel bad about it in the morning. In fact, I'd probably want to take a selfie to send to all my friends to show that I'd actually been with one of the most gorgeous men I'd ever seen in my life. And I'd seen a real movie star once.

"So actually, Mr. St. James, I was wondering if you could have the driver pull over."

"What?" he said, blinking at me in confusion. "Are you crazy?"

"No, I'm not crazy, but I think I'm going to have to get out."

"Oh gosh! The theatrics start already." He shook his head. "Don't tell me, you went to school to be an actress. You moved to LA for, what, six months or a year? You worked as a server, maybe a nanny for some rich kids who were the spawn of movie producers or directors. The dad tried to make a move on you and said, 'If you fuck me, I'll give you a bit part in my next movie.' You fucked him, you didn't get a part, and now—"

. . .

"What?" I said, gasping as I cut him off. "That's absolutely ridiculous. No, I've never wanted to be an actress. And no, I never was a nanny for anyone rich and famous. I ..."

"Then what is it? Why did you want to pull over? Wait, you want to get a burger because you're hungry?"

"No, I don't want to get a burger."

"You need to get some tampons because your time of the month just happened?"

My jaw dropped. "You're horrible. You're literally horrible. I just met you, and you're the most asinine, arrogant prick I've ever met."

.   .   .

"id you just call me a prick?" He threw his head back and started laughing, which was not the response I'd expected.

"ou think that's funny?"

"think it's hilarious. You obviously have no idea who you're dealing with."

"hat's that supposed to mean?" I said, glaring at him.

"ou obviously have no real idea how much money I'm worth. Because if you did, you wouldn't be calling me a prick. You'd be asking to see it instead."

Chapter 8

"So we're getting close to the house now. Is there anything you want to say to me before we arrive?" Noah looked at me with a raised eyebrow. I stared at him for a couple of seconds, wondering if somehow he had an inkling that I was lying. That I wasn't Annie, and that I had no experience looking after kids. I stared at him and just shook my head. "Well, actually," I said, pausing slightly, "there is one thing I want to say."

"Oh." He smirked. "And that is?"

"Well, I rather think you already know, but I'll tell you again just in case we're not on the same page."

"Go ahead."

"I have absolutely zero interest in you, Noah St. James. And when I say zero, I don't mean 0.5 or 0.01, I mean a zero. If anything, going into the negatives. I don't want to kiss you. I don't want to touch you. I don't want to sleep with you. In fact, if I don't even see you for the next thirty days, I wouldn't mind. So keep your thoughts to yourself, your hands to yourself, and your lips to yourself."

He licked his lips as he stared at me. "And are you done?"

"Excuse me?" I blinked. That was not the response I expected.

"I was wondering if you were done with that little lie." He ran his hand through his dark hair. "Here's the thing, Annie. Now that you've said that, I'm not going to touch you. I'm not going to kiss you. If any of those things are now going to happen, you'll have to beg me."

I started laughing then. "Trust me, I won't be begging you for anything. It's quite inappropriate—"

"No, it's not." He cut me off. "I don't know what sort of relationship you've been in before, but banging the brother of your employer is not inappropriate. Banging her husband would be, but as we both know, I'm not married."

"Yeah, well, I mean, you could be married for all I know because I don't know who you are."

"I'm sure when you googled me, you saw that I was one of the most eligible bachelors in the country and that I am on several top 100 40-under-40 lists around the world. You know I'm not married."

"You really think I had time to google you? Like I care." Which technically was true. I hadn't googled him because I had never even heard of him. However, if I had heard of him, I would've googled him, and I certainly was going to google him as soon as I got to the house in a private room and had Wi-Fi.

"Really? You're going to pretend?"

I put my hands up in the air. "Honest, governor," I said in my best cockney accent, "I swear on my life I haven't googled you once. And I'm not the sort of person who swears on her life if it's not true. I don't want to just drop dead."

He stared at me for a couple of seconds and nodded. "I believe you," he said. "I mean, I don't really know you, but for all intents and purposes, you do seem like an honest woman."

That made me feel slightly guilty because, in this situation, I wasn't being honest. I wasn't Annie. "So you didn't google me." He nodded. "Fair enough. And also, are you sure you don't want to be an actress?"

"I'm sure. Why are you asking me that?"

"You sure did put on a good cockney accent just now."

"Well, I think most people who try to pretend they're British talk in a cockney accent."

He laughed then. "I do find that to be true. They

either talk in a cockney accent or a very posh accent as if those were the only two British accents that existed."

I laughed then. "You seem to know a lot about British accents and people who do impersonations."

"I was in the drama club when I was in college." He chuckled. "I know, I know, you're surprised. I was only in it for a semester, and yes, it was because of a girl. It wasn't my thing, but I met a lot of thespians."

"Cool," I said, nodding, and I was surprised. I wouldn't have thought he'd taken a drama class for one day, let alone one semester. "And I remind you of these thespians that you met?" I asked him curiously.

"You do. You're quirky and fun and a little bit outlandish and over the top."

"You don't even know me," I said quickly. "How can I be all of those things?"

"I've known you long enough to know that you're playful, and that even though you're pretending to be very offended at the fact I made a move on you, you're actually quite excited and delighted."

"I wouldn't say that," I insisted. "I—"

"Your face gives you away, Annie. I mean Taytum." He frowned. "Sorry, it's going to take me a while to get used to that."

"It's okay. I just told you today that's what I preferred to be called."

"Yeah." He nodded. "Well, I'm just saying that I think my niece and nephews will really enjoy having you as their nanny."

"Great. I will enjoy being their nanny. I'm just curious about one thing, though."

"Oh, what's that?"

"You only have one suitcase with you."

"Yeah. I didn't need more than one suitcase."

"Well, you sent an email making sure we'd have plenty of space in the trunk because you said you were bringing an extra suitcase full of books that you love and other educational materials that your students found fun to work with."

I stared at him for a couple of seconds. What the hell? Who was this Annie person? Was she crazy? Who went to a job for thirty days and took school activities? It wasn't like I was a tutor or she was supposed to be a tutor. It was the Christmas holidays. Way to ruin their holidays. Now that I thought about it, the kids were lucky that I was coming instead. I would play games with them and go swimming and go shopping and eat lots of delicious food. I mean, even if I didn't get a per diem, I could afford to treat them to burgers and fries. I mean, I was getting paid a hundred, no, $100,000 for a month, so I could afford to be super generous. And I mean, it wasn't like kids ate caviar and oysters. They'd want happy meals and stuff like that. It would be absolutely amazing. "Yeah. Well, I decided that I wasn't going to bring everything I own because, you know, I'm only going to be here for one month. I didn't want it to be completely ridiculous. But I brought some art supplies, and I'm sure the kids will love that."

"Oh, art supplies." He frowned lightly. "What sort of art supplies?"

"Watercolors mainly, though colored pens as well. I do do some oil and some acrylic, but I'm mainly known for my watercolors."

"Oh," he said curiously. "Really?"

"Yeah. I'm known for my whimsical animals: foxes and bears and squirrels." I beamed at him. "In fact, I thought I was going to get a commission to—" I froze as I realized what I'd just said. Fuck, I'd nearly blown my cover. "Well, anyway, will we arrive at the house soon?" I said.

Noah tilted his head to the side and looked at me for a few seconds without saying anything. I could feel my face burning red. Was he suspicious of me now? Was he about to ask me, "Are you Taytum? Did you kill Annie?" Oh boy. I was in over my head. I really wasn't made for lying.

Chapter 9

We pulled up outside a large Victorian house just in time, and my jaw dropped. It was picture-perfect. Brick with a nice white picket fence. Flowers adorned the entire front of the yard. The front door was large and oval, and I felt like I was in a fairy tale. "Wow," I said. "This is gorgeous."

Noah turned to me and smiled, a genuine expression on his face that I realized I hadn't seen previously. "I love it here," he said. "My siblings and I grew up here, and it's my childhood home. My parents have lived here forever. It has a real sense of family." He shook his head slightly. "And there's just one other thing you should know."

"Yes. What is it?" I said, holding my breath. This was it. He was going to tell me he knew that I wasn't Annie and to get out of the car and find my way back to the train station because I was a disgraceful person for lying.

"I was just joking with you."

"Sorry? What?" I blinked at him in confusion.

"I was just joking with you. I'm not going to make a move on you, so you don't have to worry about it."

"What?" I said, still not comprehending.

"I was testing you. I wanted to see if you'd fall for it. I wanted to see if you were here just to snatch me or entrap me."

"You thought I came all this way to entrap you?"

He nodded. "You wouldn't be the first woman who's tried, and usually, they go through the bedroom route. I'm a man. You're a beautiful woman, so I wouldn't have blamed you. But you have to remember that this season, this whole gathering is for our family to come together and celebrate."

"I didn't think it was for any other reason," I said, really irritated and annoyed.

"Good," he said. "And you passed the test."

"You were testing me. What? How?"

"Well, if you would've tried to get onto my lap or kiss me or tell me to come to your bedroom tonight, I would've known that you were here for me and not the kids."

I blinked at him. "So all those things you were

saying about liking to have fun and wanting to make a move and teasing and..." I paused, feeling stupid. "That was all a test? You didn't mean any of it?"

"Exactly." He nodded. "And you passed, so we don't have to worry about it. You don't have to worry that I will sneak into your bedroom to catch a glimpse of you in your pajamas or negligee or—"

I stared at him, my lips trembling slightly. "A negligee?" I couldn't stop myself from laughing. "Why on earth would I be wearing a negligee?"

"Well, if you were hoping to seduce me."

"But I don't even know you. Why would I be trying to seduce you?"

"Taytum, I know you're not that gullible. It's an age-old trick. Young woman sees handsome, charming, rich man and tries to make a play for him."

I stared at him and just burst into laughter. I was laughing so hard that tears almost fell out of my eyes. He frowned then. "What's so funny?"

"You are. You seriously really think you're a big deal, don't you?"

"No, I don't think I'm a big deal. I—

"Yeah, maybe someone told you. Maybe you're in a newspaper article. Maybe other women have tried to seduce you and get with you, Noah St. James, but frankly, I don't care. I'm not interested in you. You're not my type."

"I'm not your type?" He raised one eyebrow and stared at me with a sardonic look on his face. "Really? You don't like handsome, rich men?"

"Um, that's not what I look for in a man. So no, I'm not interested, and you don't have to worry. And I'm glad I don't have to worry, either. If I'm honest, I've already got someone else."

"You've got someone else?"

"Yeah. And he was going to propose this Christmas." The lie slipped off my lips too easily. I chewed on my lower lip. For some reason, it felt worse than all the other lies. Maybe because it was so untrue that it was laughable. Not only did I have no one, but he sure wasn't about to propose. My boyfriend, the man I thought I would spend the rest of my life with, had ditched me and hadn't even let me know. And the worst part of it all was his new girlfriend was going home to meet his family and not me. I could feel myself wanting to cry. It was all too much now. I wasn't that strong.

"Hey, are you okay?" Noah stared at me with a warm expression on his face. "I'm sorry if I upset you. If you weren't planning on seducing me, then that's really my bad for assuming that you were going to."

"Your bad?" I said, wiping my eyes lightly.

"Yeah, my bad."

"Don't tell me that's something else you learned from your niece and nephews." I giggled.

"No." He shook his head. "I actually learned it from one of my assistants."

"Oh, okay. Because—"

"I know," he said, "I don't look like the sort of man who will say 'my bad.' But I find you'll be surprised by me, Taytum. I'm not just—"

"I know, you're not just a good-looking, handsome, rich man, et cetera, et cetera."

He smiled then. "Do I really come off like that?"

"A little bit." I nodded. "And we just met. So if I think you come off like that and we just met, I can't imagine what other people must think."

He smiled at me. "I like that you're so honest. I think I've mentioned that before."

"Yeah, you have. But I wouldn't say I'm the most honest person in the world. I mean, not that I'm a liar," I said quickly, "but all of us tell a little white lie sometimes. You know? I mean, I wouldn't tell a lie that I thought was going to hurt someone or endanger anyone. I really wouldn't. Would I tell a lie that I thought could help me in the long run, and if I thought it wouldn't do any harm? Yeah. And would I regret telling that lie? Maybe, probably. But would I admit to that lie? I—"

"It's okay." He held his hand up. "We don't have

to have a ten-minute discussion on lies. I thought you'd like to go inside and meet everyone." He frowned slightly. "Though my younger brother is not going to be there yet."

"Oh, okay."

"Which is surprising to me because he was on the train with you. But instead of him deciding to catch a ride with us, he has decided to run an errand before he gets home." He shrugged. "I have no idea what that's about, but I don't question my siblings and their decisions, no matter how idiotic they seem."

"Oh, your brother was on the train?" I asked. He nodded. I chewed on my lower lip.

Shit. I mean, he couldn't be related to Donovan, could he? I didn't think so. They didn't look alike, but what if they had a different parent? And knowing my luck, he was related to Donovan, and I would be outed. And Donovan would probably call the police because he'd think I lied just to get close to him when it had absolutely nothing to do with him.

"Are you okay, Taytum? You've gotten very white," he said. "Are you feeling sick?"

"Not sick," I said. "I get car sick sometimes, but it will be okay. Can I ask you a quick question?" I smiled at him winningly, pretending I wasn't about to faint.

"Of course. What is it?"

"Your brother, his name isn't..." I bit down on my lower lip. "Donovan, is it?" He stared at me and shook his head.

"No. No Donovan here. Why?"

"No reason," I said quickly.

Chapter 10

I wanted to burst into song. I wanted to sing Christmas carols. The Lord still loved me because I knew that Donovan would've been Noah's brother if he was super mad at me, and I would've been out on my ear faster than I could blink. "Shall we go inside?" I said, suddenly feeling happy.

"Sure," he said. "I'm more than happy to." He opened his door and got out, and I sat there wondering if I should open my door as well. I noticed that John was walking around to my side, so I decided to let him open it for me. I knew I was the help and shouldn't expect to be treated like some sort of A-list star or member of royalty. But I found it chivalrous when men opened the door for me, and I was the sort of girl who admired chivalry. I liked it when guys opened car doors and regular doors for me. I liked it when they pulled out my chair so I could have a seat. I liked it when they offered me a drink before they drank themselves. I liked it if they offered me their coat.

"Ma'am, we've arrived," John said as he opened the door and smiled at me.

"Thank you," I said as I got out. "I'm sorry I don't have any cash, or I would've tipped you," I said quickly, and John chuckled.

"No need for a tip, ma'am." And he offered me a little bow. "Welcome to your home for the holiday season."

"It's beautiful." I looked around. "Do you live in town as well?"

He nodded. "The St. James family graciously bought me a little cottage about ten minutes from here. I live there with my wife."

"Oh wow. That's amazing."

"It's lovely," he said. "They're a lovely family. I'm sure you'll love working for them. And who knows, maybe if you want to, of course, they'll offer you an annual position."

"Oh, well, I don't know about that," I said quickly. I mean, I like kids, and I like to make money, but I didn't think I wanted to be a nanny full-time. I mean, for a month and a lot of money? Sure. For a year? No. Plus, I didn't really know what to do with kids. I figured I could fake it for thirty days, but I could not fake it for a year.

"Well, just think about it, ma'am. I just wanted to let you know that normally the Christmas nanny gets an offer with the family if she does a good job."

"Oh, well, that's great to know. Thank you." I smiled at him.

"Are you ready, Taytum?" Noah looked at me as I stood there chatting with John.

"Yeah, I'm ready. Thank you." I gave him a warm smile even though I still wasn't quite sure what I thought about Noah St. James.

"This way." He walked toward the front of the house and opened the small white picket gate for me. I looked to the left and the right, and I could see beautiful holly and ivy framing the entrance.

"I feel like I'm entering an English cottage," I said as I walked through. "I mean, not really a cottage because it's so big, more like a manor house or something."

He started laughing then but didn't respond. "Come on. I'm sure my parents are excited to see you. They'll probably have some cider or mulled wine ready for us."

"Ooh, do you think they'll have eggnog?"

"Eggnog?" He made a face. "We're not quite in eggnog territory, are we?"

"Well, it is a Christmas drink."

"True. But my family tends to drink it only on Christmas Eve and Christmas Day."

"Oh, okay."

"But I'm sure if you really like it, we could arrange to have it on hand for you during your stay here."

"Oh no," I said quickly. "You really don't have to go out of your way. I—"

"Trust me. We'll just add it to the weekly grocery list." He smiled. "It's fine."

"Thanks, Noah." I gave him a warm smile. I was really starting to like him. Maybe he wasn't so bad after all.

"I think it's better if you call me Mr. St. James," he said, and my jaw dropped.

"Sorry, what?" I wasn't sure if he was joking.

"Just for professional reasons," he said, nodding. "You know?"

"You want me to call you Mr. St. James?"

"Yes. Why? Is that going to be a problem?"

"No, but…" I bit down on my lower lip. He was a jerk. I had been right the entire time. Mr. St. James? He wanted me to call him Mr. St. James? What? Was he joking? It's not like he was my principal or my boss or anyone really, really important. I mean, granted, he was technically my boss because he was the one signing my paycheck, but I wasn't going to be answering to him. He wasn't the father of the children. He was just the uncle. And—

"Come on, Taytum. And by the way, you don't want to catch a fly."

"Sorry? Catch a fly with what?"

"Your mouth," he said, pointing at my lips.

"What are you talking about, Mr. St. James?" I glared at him.

"If you leave your mouth hanging open, you'll catch flies. But I don't know, maybe you're like that old lady who likes to swallow flies."

"Maybe I'm like the old lady who likes to swallow flies?" I gawked at him. "What are you talking about?"

"You've never heard that rhyme?" He grinned. "I know an old lady who swallowed a fly. I don't know why she swallowed a fly. Perhaps she'll die."

My eyes narrowed, and I stared at him. "Are you calling me old?"

He started laughing then. "Why do women always assume that every little comment is about their age?"

"Well, you just said I remind you of this rhyme, and the rhyme is about knowing an old lady."

"Well, I was just seeing if you knew it. I know an old lady who swallowed a fly. She…" He paused. "Wait, I think I got the next part wrong." I stared at him for a couple of seconds as he thought hard. I shook my head and did a little dance before continuing.

"I know an old lady who swallowed a spider that wiggled and jiggled and tickled inside her. She swallowed the spider to catch the fly. I don't know why she swallowed a fly. Perhaps she'll die," I said, and he stared at me with wide eyes.

"So you do know the rhyme."

"Of course I do. I work with kids, after all," I said quickly. I meant to say that I'm an illustrator for children's books, so I know quite a lot about children's rhymes, but I didn't say that.

"I know an old lady who swallowed a bird. She swallowed the bird to catch the spider, which wiggled and jiggled and tickled inside her. She swallowed the spider to catch the fly. I don't know why she swallowed a fly. Perhaps she'll die." He stared at me.

"I know an old lady who swallowed a cat," I said, winking at him, and he chuckled. "She swallowed the cat to catch the bird. She swallowed the bird to catch the spider, which wiggled and jiggled and tickled inside her. She swallowed the spider to catch the fly. I don't know why she swallowed a fly. Perhaps she'll die."

"I know an old lady who swallowed a dog," he said, grinning. "She swallowed the dog to catch the cat." He paused as the front door opened.

"Noah, there you are, son!" A tall, older man

with wise blue eyes came down the steps. "Oh, your mother will be so happy that you're finally here." He walked over to Noah and gave him a quick hug. "So good to see you."

"Hey, Pops," Noah said, hugging his dad back. "This is Annie, also known as Taytum. She's going to be the nanny for the Christmas season."

Noah's father stepped back and looked me over. He had a warm, genuine look on his face. "Nice to meet you, Annie, also known as Taytum." He smiled and laughed. "Welcome to the family. We're very glad to have you."

Chapter 11

We walked inside the house, and I couldn't stop myself from beaming with happiness. It was weird, but as I looked around the entryway and stared at the tinsel and the Christmas decorations hanging on the wall, I felt like I was home. This was the sort of place I'd always imagined myself spending Christmas. My parents weren't really fond of decorating and barely put up a tree when I was a kid, but I'd always dreamed of a much more celebratory holiday season.

"Let me introduce you to my wife, Taytum," Noah's dad said as we walked through the corridor. "She's probably in the kitchen baking gingerbread cookies."

"Oh, yummy," I said, smiling as I followed him.

"Well, I'm going to my room. I have some calls to

make," Noah said. He looked at me with a dismissive nod, and I nodded back. I watched as he put his hand on his dad's back. "Catch up with you later, okay, Pops?"

"Sounds good. Don't work too hard, son."

"I always do." Noah laughed. And I watched as he walked away. I felt a little bit sad that he was leaving. There was something about the way that he looked at me and the way that he made me feel that I was loathsome to lose.

"So Annie, I mean Taytum," Noah's dad said with a small smile, "the kids call me Pop Pop, and you can feel free to call me Pop Pop as well."

"Oh, thank you. That's a really cute name."

"Yeah, I kind of like it." He nodded. "Lulu has just gone to the shops with the kids, but they should be back soon."

"Oh, okay." I bit down on my lower lip. Who was Lulu when she was at home? Not that I can say that to him. Then it hit me. If Lulu was with the kids, Lulu had to be the kids' mother, right? "She was so nice when we spoke on the phone, and I'm so happy she offered me this position," I said quickly, crossing my fingers, hoping I got it right.

"Yeah, she's really excited to meet you as well." He nodded. "So, honey, look who's here."

A beautiful older woman looked up from the island in the middle of the kitchen. Her hands were covered with flour, and I could see some flour on her cheeks as well. She beamed at me. "Oh, you must be Annie. So wonderful to meet you, dear."

"Hi, I'm Annie, but I go by Taytum. It's my middle name, but everyone actually calls me Taytum because I have a cousin called Annie, and when we were younger, our parents didn't want us to—"

"It's fine. I love the name Taytum. Reminds me of one of my favorite actresses, Tatum O'Neal."

I stared at her and grinned. "Actually, my mom loved Tatum O'Neal as well. She loved Ryan O'Neal from that movie *Love Story*. She had a crush on him. And when he named his child Tatum, she said she was—" I bit down on my lower lip. Stop going on, I chided myself. "Sorry. I like to babble."

"Don't worry, dear. Would you like a gingerbread man?" She held up what appeared to be a recently decorated gingerbread man. It looked delicious.

"Ooh. I wouldn't say no to that," I said as I walked toward her.

"And would you like some tea or coffee to go with that? Or I could make some hot chocolate or—"

"Coffee would be great." I nodded. "Actually, it's late. I don't know if I should have coffee."

"Yes. Maybe some hot chocolate, then?"

"Yeah." I frowned slightly.

"What is it, dear?"

"Oh, I was just surprised that Lulu took the kids to the store this late."

"Oh, they wanted a toy, and she does spoil them so, so she said, 'Come on, let's go.' I think she's hoping that all the activity will wear them out, and they'll sleep through the night."

"Sleep through the night? But they're not babies, right?"

"No, they're not babies. But they do like to get up." She looked over at her husband. "But I'm sure you'll be able to help with that. Lulu told me you've dealt with children with nighttime issues?"

I stared at her for a couple of seconds. What did I say to that? Maybe the real Annie did have that experience, but I didn't even know what nighttime issues meant. Were they peeing the bed? Were they having nightmares? Were they sleepwalking? I decided the best response was no response and bit down into the gingerbread cookie. "Mmm, this is so delicious," I said, licking my lips. "Wow, you are an absolutely amazing cook. Do you have, like, a cookie store or something?"

Pop Pop started laughing. "No, but I always tell her she should open a bakery."

"I don't have time to open a bakery, dear. Not now that I'm looking after all my children and—"

"All your children are grown, darling." Pop Pop shook his head. "I know that you would love to open a little village store, and I know that everyone in town would love you to as well."

"But, darling—"

"But, darling, nothing. The boys are all grown. And yes, Lulu still acts like a child, and we have the grandkids, but..." He paused and looked at me. "Sorry. This is just a conversation we have yearly. My wife has always wanted to have a little bakery, but she's been so focused on bringing up the kids, which I was very thankful for because it meant a warm meal was always on the table when I got home. And the boys were always fed and clean, and we didn't have to worry about trusting them in someone else's care." He froze suddenly. "Oh sorry, I didn't mean to say that."

"It's okay," I said. "I don't take offense to that. I know it's very hard to find trustworthy babysitters and nannies." I tried not to make a face. I was the sort of person he was worried about. I was a liar and a fraud. I needed to leave the house. I shouldn't be here. This was a really nice, loving, caring family, and... I was deceiving them and not even for a good reason. And while some people might think money was a good reason, I didn't. I'd just let everything overwhelm me and gone with it because Noah had been such a jerk at first. But now I realized I was in the wrong, and there was no excuse. I couldn't pretend to be a nanny if it meant lying to these wonderful, kindhearted people.

The door opened suddenly, and I almost jumped out of my skin. I wasn't sure why I was so jumpy. Maybe because I was in the middle of a huge lie and scared shitless that I would get caught. "Hey, hey, hey, I'm home." It was a deep voice, and I stood there wondering who it could be.

"We're in the kitchen," Pop Pop shouted, and I heard footsteps clanking on the ground as whoever it was made his way to the kitchen. And there stood a slightly younger, even more gorgeous version of Noah.

"Hey, everyone." He grinned, his blue eyes crinkling as he smiled at me. "Hey, Pop Pop. Hey, Mom." He walked over and gave them a big hug that seemed to last forever. They really were a close family. He walked over to me and held out his hand. "Nice to meet you. I'm Dylan. Dylan St. James. I'm the third oldest brother."

"Hi, I'm Taytum. I'm—" I bit down on my lower lip. This was the time to make the decision. "I'm the holiday nanny."

Chapter 12

My heart raced as I stared into Dylan St. James's blue eyes. He had a warm smile on his face, which made me like him more than his brother. I couldn't believe how lucky I was to be spending Christmas with two handsome men. I couldn't wait to call Danielle and tell her all about it. Especially Noah. He was such a hottie. I swallowed hard as I heard footsteps and looked to see Noah entering the room as if he could read my mind. He walked into the kitchen casually as if he were here almost by mistake. He was frowning as he stared at me.

"Shouldn't you be working, Taytum?" he said, a snip in his voice.

"Sorry, what?" I blinked at him as I looked at him and then back at Dylan.

Dylan rolled his eyes and walked over to me.

"Don't mind my brother. He's a slave master. He absolutely can't stand to see anyone just relaxing and having fun."

"Very funny, Dylan." Noah shook his head. "Good to see you, though."

"Good to see you too, big bro and dominator of the world."

"I haven't dominated the world," Noah said. But I could tell he looked pleased by the comment. So he really was into business. I decided that I definitely wasn't going to out myself at that moment. The last thing I needed was for Noah St. James to go off on me after everything we'd already gone through.

"So Annie," Dylan said, "I hear that—"

"Please call me Taytum. And it sounds like your sister, Lulu, has really been singing my praises. And while I really appreciate that, it does make me feel a little bit awkward. I'm a modest sort of girl, and…" I paused and looked over at Pop Pop, who was grinning at me. "Well, anyway, just to say, I don't love talking about myself. I'd much rather get to know the family, and I can't wait to meet the kids." I beamed.

Noah headed over to the fridge and grabbed a beer. "You want one, Dylan?"

"Won't say no."

"Well, do I not get a hug from you, son?" Noah's mom looked over at him, and he started laughing.

"Sorry, Mom, I—"

"I know. You were busy with work, and now you're busy with your beer, but—"

"But nothing. I should have come and given you a kiss and a hug first," he said. "So any dinner left?"

"Yes, I made your favorite."

"What's your favorite?" I asked curiously.

"Pot roast." He grinned. I was surprised.

"Pot roast and mashed potatoes," Pop Pop said.

"Yep. I'm just like you, Dad," Noah said with a smile.

"Wow. I never would've guessed that was your favorite meal."

"Oh," he said. "What would you have guessed?"

"I don't know. Canapes, uh, champagne and caviar, tuna tartare, something like that."

"I mean, I do like tuna tartare, but would I have it on my deathbed? Probably not." He shook his head.

"Not that you asked me." Dylan sidled up next to me and smiled warmly into my eyes. "But I like steak."

"I like a good steak too," I beamed, wondering how two brothers could have such opposite personalities.

"Yeah. Well, no one asked you, like you said, Dylan," Noah said. "Where's everyone else? Where's Lulu? Where are the kids?"

"Lulu took the kids to the store so they could get some toys."

Noah frowned and looked at his watch. "At this time? Really?"

Dylan cackled slightly. "What? Come on, now. She's a St. James. Don't we all solve problems with gifts?"

"No, we don't." Noah frowned at his brother. And I wondered what that was about. It seemed like there was some sort of history there. And me, being the nosy person, I wanted to know exactly what history that was.

"Noah, why don't you show Taytum her room, please?" his mom asked gently. "And I'll heat you up some dinner?" She looked over at me. "Are you hungry as well, Taytum? Would you like some?"

"I definitely wouldn't say no"—I nodded—"if that's okay."

"Of course. And you, Dylan?"

"Mom, I'll always eat your food."

"I'll have some more," Pop Pop said. And she just stared at him.

"Really? You already had two servings."

"And now I will have my third." He grinned, and I laughed.

Noah walked over to me. "Come on, I'll show you to your room, Taytum."

"Thank you," I said. "Well, it was good meeting everyone, and I will be back down soon."

"Yeah, come back down in about twenty minutes. Everything should be ready then." Noah's mom nodded and smiled at me. "Welcome to our home, Taytum. I really hope you have an enjoyable Christmas season with us. I know how hard it must be for you to be away from your family during the holidays."

"Oh, thank you," I said warmly. "My parents went to the Caribbean"—I shrugged—"so it would've just been me. So I don't mind. And you have such a gorgeous house and such a large, warm, happy family. I'm sure I'll have the best experience. Like a Hallmark movie picture-perfect Christmas."

Dylan started laughing then. "There's absolutely nothing Hallmark picture-perfect about our family. Don't let the glitzy house fool you."

Pop Pop shook his head. "Don't mind him, Taytum. My sons, you'll find, are very spoiled and very opinionated, but we do have a very warm, loving family."

"I didn't say it wasn't warm and loving," Dylan said. "I was just saying that—" He pressed his lips together. "Well anyway, welcome, Taytum. I, for one, am very glad you're here, and I look forward to getting to know you a lot better."

"Thanks," I said. "I look forward to getting to know you too."

"Come on," Noah said gruffly. "We don't have time for you two to be flirting up a storm. There's work to be done."

I bit down on my lower lip and watched as the other family members looked at each other but didn't say anything. Noah walked out of the kitchen, and I gave them a small wave as I followed him. "What is your problem?" I said to Noah as we made our way up the staircase.

"I just want to remind you that you're here for a job. I know that my brother is very attractive, and you might think you're here to have fun and do whatever you nannies think you're going to do when you work for a rich family. But I just want you to know that my brother is a playboy. And if you think that he's—"

"I'm going to stop you right there, Noah," I said, irritation clear in my voice. "I've already told you that I'm not here to trap or get with you or your brothers. You even said that you weren't even interested in having a relationship or anything sexual with me and that you were just testing me, and you said that I passed the test. So what is this all about?"

"You may have passed the test with me, but I'm not an easy mark like my brother Dylan. You're a pretty girl, and you probably can—"

"I'm going to stop you again, Noah. You're a jackass. I mean, when I first met you, which wasn't even that long ago, I thought you were a jackass. Then I thought, maybe he's not as bad as I thought, but my initial and first opinion of you was correct. You absolutely suck. Who do you think you're talking to? I'm not going to accept this. And the sooner you realize that, the better. I'm only here to work for your family to help you. Okay? And I'm giving up a lot to do that. So just don't think that you can—" I sputtered. His eyes changed as he glanced at me, and I could see him moving forward. "What are you doing?" I said as I froze.

Chapter 13

Noah's lips pressed against mine, and I gasped as my eyes widened. There was a devious glint in his as he pulled back slightly. "What did you just do?" I said, my breath raspy, my heart racing.

"I think I just gave you a peck," he said, winking at me.

"B... But why did you do that?" I said, squeaking.

"I'm sorry. I thought you wanted me to."

"But we were literally just arguing. Why did you think I—"

His lips pressed down on me again, and I almost moaned as I felt his arms wrapping around my waist and pulling me into him. Involuntarily, I reached up and grabbed the side of his face and ran my fingers through his dark hair. I pressed my lips against him and kissed him back. I knew I shouldn't. I knew I was being an idiot, but I couldn't resist. His lips felt so good against mine, and his body was warm and hard. And the way his fingertips were pressed into my waist made me feel womanly and sexy. His fingers ran down to my ass and squeezed slightly. And I moaned as he pulled me into him harder, and I felt something pressed against my stomach. I knew exactly what it was, and it made me feel alive and even more sexier than ever. He pulled away. This time, there was no devious glint in his eyes, but pure lust.

"I take it you enjoyed that, Taytum?" he said, staring into my eyes as if willing me to say otherwise.

"Of course." I couldn't lie. Of course I'd enjoyed it. I wanted him to kiss me again. In fact, I wanted him to lead me to his bedroom and throw me down on the mattress and have his wicked way with me. I wanted him to act like some big bad wolf and devour me. But of course I would never say that. And if he could read my mind, I would pretend he was reading it incorrectly because there was no way I wanted to admit it. I licked my lips quickly. "I think that you are…" My brain was foggy. I didn't know what to say.

"I'm waiting, Taytum," he said. His eyes crinkled as he gazed at my lips. He still hadn't removed his fingers from my waist, and I hadn't stepped back from his hardness. I enjoyed the swell of it against me. "Still waiting," he said again.

"I... I can't remember what I was going to say." Which was true. Words had left me. I just wanted for this moment to be frozen in time because the way he made me feel, the way my entire body was electrified was unlike anything I'd ever felt in my life. And I knew I would be in trouble because if he kissed me again, I wouldn't be able to say no. And if he teased me and tantalized me and asked me to beg him, I had a feeling I would because I had no shame. Chasing after Donovan and catching the train showed me that. And Noah St. James? Well, he was a hundred times better looking than Donovan and had a million times more charisma and sex appeal.

Noah St. James was the sort of man who could make you drop your panties with one glance. And I wasn't embarrassed to admit that I wanted to drop my panties right now. Of course I wouldn't tell him that. And it's not like I would reach up and pull them down. But if I had some alcohol in me, and we were in a nightclub or something, I had a feeling that something pretty dirty would likely be going on, which would only further complicate everything. I felt like Alice in Wonderland, going deeper and deeper into a hole with no way out. I wasn't quite sure what I was doing or why I was doing it. And the allure of money wasn't even making it seem right. I needed to speak to Danielle because even though she was flighty and capricious and a daydreamer herself, she still had common sense. And she would tell me what to do in this situation. And if she told me to pack up my bags and leave, I would. Frankly, I was lucky because I hadn't even unpacked yet.

"I think I'd like you to show me to my room, please," I said softly, biting down on my lower lip. That wasn't what I wanted to say. I wanted to say, 'Take me now, Noah St. James. Do your best.' But I knew that I would regret it. Maybe not the sex, because I had a feeling it was going to be hot, but maybe just the entire situation. Because I knew if I said to Noah St. James, 'Take me now and have your wicked way with me,' he'd say something like, 'I knew you couldn't resist,' or, 'I told you you'd want me.' And as much as that was true, I didn't want him to be right. I didn't want him to be smug. I didn't want him to think that it was part of my elaborate plan to hook up with him and then make a bid for his money. As if.

"Okay." He nodded. "Let me take you to your room. I do want you to know that it's next door to mine," he said as he let go of me, and we continued to make our way up the stairs.

"Okay, that's good." I shrugged.

"And there's a connecting door." He grinned.

"Wait, what? What do you mean there's a connecting door?"

"Well, we have a jack and jill bathroom." He smirked. "So we'll be sharing a bathroom. And as you can probably guess, there's a door from your room to the bathroom, and there's a door from my room to the bathroom. So we can meet in the middle."

"But we don't have to," I said, blinking at him.

"We don't have to, of course." He grinned. "But I think you'll want to."

"I think you think way too much of yourself."

"Okay, then. Let me ask you one question."

"Ask away," I said, blinking at him. "What's the question?"

"Did you enjoy that kiss?"

I stared at him for a couple of seconds. "I studied history and government in high school and college," I said to him.

"Okay. And?" He looked confused.

"So I know I can plead the Fifth."

He chuckled. "You do know that pleading the Fifth gives me the answer anyway."

I shrugged. "You can think what you want to think. It may be that it was fun, or it may be that I don't want to hurt your feelings because you seem like you're hypermasculine and hyper controlling and hypersensitive and hyper full of yourself. And I don't know if you could handle the fact that I might not have thought it was all that."

He laughed even harder then. "Oh my. Taytum, Taytum, Taytum. Do you think that makes me doubt myself?"

"No, but it should."

He grinned. "I bet you, before the week is out, I'll have you in my bed screaming and begging me to take you. And you know what?" he said softly as we stopped outside a door.

"No. What?" I looked up at him.

"I will only take you once you admit to me just how great of a kisser I am and just how turned on I make you."

"That's never going to happen, Noah St. James."

"Oh, I think it will," he said, smiling warmly. "I think it will happen very, very soon."

Chapter 14

"So how did you like your room?" Dylan asked me as I entered the kitchen thirty minutes later. Noah had shown me my room, then disappeared without a trace. I'd half expected him to try to seduce me then and there. In fact, I'd half hoped that he would. It was crazy, but I'd already forgotten about my hurt with Donovan. Compared to Noah, Donovan was a slimy worm. But Noah, Noah was a strong bear or wolf, alpha and sexy. Noah made me happy to be myself. He made me feel alive. He made me feel wanted. He made me feel like I was someone special.

"It's lovely," I admitted honestly, thinking back to my cozy room with his queen-sized bed covered with a cute flannel blanket. "Your parents' house is absolutely amazing. It reminds me of something on one of those reality TV shows on HGTV or something. And not the before, the after," I gushed and smiled at Pop Pop, who was in the corner of the room. He looked pleased as he gazed at me and nodded. "It really does feel like a home. My wife and I have always thought we should ensure that our house is homey and cozy and not just follow modern trends."

"Your wife and you?" Noah's mom, Nana J, smiled as she raised an eyebrow. "Honey, I believe I'm the one who made all the decisions about what should be in the home."

Pop Pop laughed then, a hearty sound that reminded me of Noah. "Well, that's true." He grinned at me. "The woman is always right. You know that, right?"

"I sure do." I laughed. "Oh my gosh, that smells absolutely delicious," I said as I smelled a whiff of the pot roast. "You put it back in the oven?" I walked over to Nana J, who was standing next to the stove.

"I did," she said. "I know some people might microwave food to warm it again, but I like to put it back in the oven. I didn't make the meat super well done, so it won't overcook when I put it back."

"Oh, cool. I don't know how you do it," I said to her. "I'm an awful cook. I try, but I'm just not good."

"But at least you're good with kids," Dylan said, coming and standing next to me. "I heard you're the Mary Poppins of New York."

I stared at him for a couple of seconds, my heart racing. I hated it when the family brought up my nanny background. It made me feel guilty every single time. I felt my face should have a sign on it that read, "FRAUD." I smiled weakly and waved my hands in the air. "Well, you know, chim chimney cher-ee," I said quickly, and he laughed.

"What's so funny?" Noah said as he entered the kitchen, looking at me with an annoyed expression. However, the look he gave Dylan seemed almost deadly. He raised a single eyebrow and came to stand next to me. "Thinking about how much money you're taking me for?"

Dylan stared at the two of us. "Really, Noah? That's rude."

"*N*oah, that is unacceptable," Pop Pop said, frowning as he chastised his son. "We do not speak to people that way. You're not too old for a whooping, son."

"Sorry." Noah grinned and shook his head. "I mean, it's not that bad if she's laughing at my joke. I'd be laughing if I was getting paid so much money to be a nanny for a month."

"Yeah, well, when you're the Mary Poppins of New York City, you can get whatever you want," I said, smiling at him sweetly. "You know, there's a family who I'm not going to name, but let's just say they are the heirs to an oil fortune. They offered to fly me to Paris to get fresh macarons every Saturday morning for the kids."

"Really?" he said, staring at me with disbelief in his eyes. "And what's the name of this family who offered you that?"

I stared at him, biting down on my lower lip. "I'm not going to tell you because—"

"Because they don't exist," Noah said, laughing.

I looked over at Dylan, who was shaking his head. "Ignore my brother. He's an idiot. He's got more money than he knows what to do with. But ask him to part with even a cent of it, and he goes on and on like he's doing you a favor. You're the one doing us a huge favor, Annie." He ran his hand through his hair as he smiled at me sincerely. "Sorry, Taytum, I mean."

"Yes, you really are such a godsend, dear," Pop Pop said. "And I can't wait for you to meet Lulu and the kids. Where can they be?" As if like clockwork, the front door opened and three small little voices carried through the hall. "Pop Pop! Pop Pop!" cried a little girl loudly. I winced slightly at how high her pitch was.

"I got a new Barbie!" she said, running into the kitchen. I stared at the little girl, her blond hair flying behind her as she ran up to Pop Pop and gave him a hug and held up her Barbie. "And I'm calling her Cindy because I like the name Cindy," she said, grinning.

"Well, hello, Cindy." Pop Pop hugged her and smiled at the doll.

Two little boys also came barreling into the room before I could introduce myself. "Pop Pop! Pop Pop!" the smallest little one said, his face smeared with chocolate. "I got a choo choo train. Choo choo!" he screamed at the top of his lungs.

Noah shook his head, and Dylan just smiled wryly. "I'm so glad you're here, Mary Poppins." He winked at me, and I nodded faintly, not knowing what to say.

*T*he other little boy looked around the kitchen, and I thought for one second that at least one of them was quiet. I should have known I wasn't going to be that lucky as just a few seconds later, he started screaming, the most blood-curdling scream I'd ever heard. "Oh my gosh, what is going on, Sammy?" Noah said, touching his nephew's shoulder.

"I wanted to get a candy cane, and Mommy didn't let me get a candy cane."

I wasn't sure if I was supposed to respond to that. Before I could say anything, a woman, who I presumed was Lulu St. James, walked into the kitchen. She looked frazzled and tired. She had two bags in her hand, and she was shaking her head. "That's not true, Sammy. You got a peppermint candy cane. I didn't let you have a second one."

"I want a candy cane!" he shouted, stomping his feet.

I bit down on my lower lip. Fuck. Was I supposed to do something to stop this hot mess? These kids were terrors. What the hell had gone on? The family all seemed sane and normal. The house was beautiful. But these kids, they were like little demon kids. These were not going to be easy kids. And now, all of a sudden, I realized why Annie, whoever she was, was getting paid or was supposed to be getting paid a hundred thousand dollars. And now I understood why the family would hire the Mary Poppins to New York because who wanted to deal with brats like this? Certainly not me.

"Lulu"—Pop Pop stepped forward—"this is Annie. She goes by Taytum. The nanny."

Lulu's eyes lit up, and she stared at me. She stepped forward and gave me a huge hug. "Oh, Annie, am I glad to see you." She stepped back for a second and observed my face. "You look different," she said, looking me up and down.

"Oh, what do you mean?" I said, biting down on my lower lip.

"When we FaceTimed, you had blond hair, and you looked a little bit chubbier," she said.

Fuck. Of course, they had FaceTimed. Why hadn't I thought about that? "I did intermittent fasting," I said quickly, "and I lost some weight. And I wasn't a natural blond, so I dyed it back to my natural color," I said, hoping that Lulu hadn't paid that much attention to Annie's features other than the superficial stuff.

"Oh, okay. How is the intermittent fasting? Was it hard? I mean, how long were you doing it for? Because you really look like you lost a lot of weight." I stared at her for a couple of seconds, not knowing if she was being facetious because I certainly wasn't super skinny.

"Um, I did it for a while," I said, not giving a timeframe because I had no idea when Lulu had interviewed Annie.

"So here are the kids in person," she said. "This is Sammy. This is Pollyanna. And this is Theo, who sometimes goes by Johnny Boy."

"Johnny Boy?" I said, raising an eyebrow.

"Well, his name is Theodore, but he likes to go by Johnny Boy right now"—she sighed—"and I'm too tired to say anything else."

"Sure, I understand that." I smiled at the kids.

"Hi, everyone, I'm Annie, but you can call me Taytum. I'm the Mary Poppins of Manhattan, and I'm going to teach you your ABCs and 1, 2, 3s and—"

Before I could even finish the sentence, all of the kids had run away, and I knew this was going to be a hot mess of a month.

Chapter 15

"Danielle, I need help," I whispered into the phone as I sat on my bed after dinner. I was finally able to call her and fill her in on what was going on. I'd tried to include Isabella in the call as well, but she hadn't answered the phone. "I'm dead meat."

"What's going on? Are Donovan's parents absolutely horrible? How did it go? Tell me everything."

"I'm not at Donovan's house," I said, hardly believing where I was myself.

"What?" she screamed into the phone. "Where are you?"

"I'm in Little Kimble, but—"

. . .

"*Y*ou're in Little Kimble, but you're not at his house? Oh my gosh, girl, do not tell me you rented a hotel room. You can't afford a hotel."

"I'm not in a hotel. I'm in a house."

"What house?"

"The residence of the St. James family."

"Whose family? What? Is that supposed to mean something to me? What is going on, Taytum? I don't understand." Danielle sounded worried. "Have you lost your mind? Did it go badly with Donovan and—"

"What makes you think it went badly with Donovan?" I asked.

"I mean, if I'm honest, I didn't think it would go brilliantly."

"Yet you still encouraged me to go."

"Because I wanted you to see that he wasn't the guy for you so you would break up with him and move on with your life. But where the hell are you now?"

"I told you I'm at the St. James family house. It's this really gorgeous house in Little Kimble and—"

"I know that's where you are, though I don't even know who they are and what you're doing there."

"I'm the Christmas nanny," I said, wanting to laugh and cry at the same time. There was silence on the other end of the phone. "Danielle, are you still there?"

"I'm still here," she said slowly. "I thought you just said you were the Christmas nanny."

"I am the Christmas nanny."

"Girl, what in the hell is going on?"

I sighed. "Long story short, it didn't work out with Donovan. He didn't want me to come and surprise him on the train. He didn't want me to meet his parents for Christmas. He didn't even want to be with me because he had another woman."

"Oh shit. He was cheating on you?"

"I guess so. So to save face, I pretended I was this girl Annie because this guy came up to me with a sign. He's like, 'Are you Annie the Christmas nanny?' And Donovan was right behind me with his little bitch of a whore girlfriend. And so I was like, 'Yeah, I'm the nanny.' And I planned on just getting into the back of the limo and being driven for a couple of blocks, and then I'd be like, 'Oh my gosh. Did you say Annie? I thought you said Taytum.' But—"

Danielle cleared her throat. "Taytum, you are confusing the heck out of me. What?"

"So anyway, I get into the back of the limo, and there's this gorgeous yet irritating grumpy asshole, and he was all like, 'You're late.' And I was all like, 'Excuse you, you jackass.' I mean, I didn't really say that, but I was thinking that. And—"

"Who was in the back of the limo? Some pimp?" Danielle sounded more confused than I'd ever heard her in her life.

"No." I laughed. "His name's Noah. Noah St. James. He's the eldest son in the St. James family, and—"

"And so what? You're going to be a nanny to his kids or something? What, is he like Scrooge?"

"No, I'm not going to be a nanny to his kids. I'm going to be a nanny to his sister's kids. Lulu."

"Okay. Continue," she said. "But they didn't think it was suspicious when you said, 'I'm not Annie, I'm Taytum'?"

"No, I kind of said my name was really Taytum."

"So they just believed you?"

"I mean, I said my name was Annie, but I go by Taytum because that's my middle name and—"

"Oh gosh. So you lied."

"Yeah, a little."

"Girl, what are you doing? You don't know anything about kids."

"Trust me. I'm realizing that now. The kids are brats, girl, and I don't know what to do. There's no way in hell I'm going to be able to control these three hellions for even a day, let alone a month."

"Taytum, just catch the next train and come home. What's stopping you?"

"Because—"

"Oh shit. Do you not have any money? Look, I can rent a car and come up and get you if you want."

"You're such a good friend, Danielle. But no, I might try to stay."

"Why?"

"Because the pay is super good."

"Girl, you can get a job in New York. I'm sure Macy's is hiring. They're always hiring in the Christmas season."

"Is Macy's going to pay me a hundred thousand dollars for one month?"

"Shut up," she said, gasping in shock.

"Yep," I said, grinning.

"Who did you say these people were? The Carnegies?"

"No." I laughed. "The St. Jameses."

"Who are the St. Jameses, and why haven't I heard of them?" she said. "And… wait, did you say Noah St. James is like hunky? Are you interested in him? Oh my God. Do you have a hot new billionaire boyfriend because I told you to go on that train ride?"

"He's not my boyfriend, and I don't know if he's a billionaire. Though I'm sure he must be close to one if he can afford to pay me a hundred grand for the Christmas season."

"Yeah. And you said he was cute."

"Yeah, he's cute, but he's such a jackass."

"Um, didn't you just meet him tonight?"

"Yeah. And?"

"So how do you know he's a jackass?"

"*B*ecause he's got that pompous, 'I'm super rich, and I can tell you what to do, and I'm your boss' attitude."

"He is your boss, though."

"I mean, kind of."

She sighed. "What happens when the real Annie shows up?"

I paused then. "So I was thinking about this a little bit and—"

"And what?"

"I figured I would say there had been a mix-up."

"What? What are you talking about, Taytum? What mix-up?"

"I would say that I was also hired to work for a St. James family in Little Kimble, and that I must have misunderstood and gotten the wrong family."

"Girl, who the hell is going to believe that?"

"I don't know," I said, laughing, "but I mean, maybe Annie is not coming. She certainly didn't get off the train, and no one's heard from her."

"Girl, shall I rent a car tomorrow and come get you?"

"No, you don't have to do that. I was still going to try to see if it could work out."

"But you don't know anything about kids."

"I know. And honestly, it's not even about the money. But—"

"But what? Out with it, Taytum."

"Noah kind of kissed me and—"

"Oh my gosh! He kissed you? When? Where and—"

"What do you mean where?" I said, cutting her off.

"Like where did he kiss you? In the car, in the house, in the…" She paused. "What did you think I meant?"

"Oh, I thought you meant like where on my body did he kiss me." She started laughing out loud then.

"Girl, are you crazy?"

"What?" I asked. "That could have been what you were asking."

"You literally just met the man today. Did you really think I was going to ask you if he was kissing your vagina?"

. . .

I giggled. "No. But hey, maybe he wanted to."

"I'm sure he wanted to. Every man wants to, but that doesn't mean we let them, not on a first…" She paused. "I was going to say date, but that was just a meeting, right?"

"Yeah."

"So how did this kiss happen?"

"He was showing me to my room and—"

"Oh Lord. Taytum, this is starting to sound like something out of a cheesy romance movie or the beginning of a horror movie."

"It's neither," I said. "And anyway, remember I wanted my Hallmark Christmas."

"Yeah, but—"

"But nothing. He was showing me to my room, and we kind of had this moment on the stairs when he kissed me, and I kind of kissed him back. And he was…" I paused and giggled.

"He was what?" she asked.

"He was super aroused, and I could feel it against my stomach. And he's kind of hard, like big and hard, if you know what I mean."

"Oh girl." She started laughing then. "I know exactly what you mean. Not that I've had anything big and hard recently, unless you count the dildo that

I bought a couple of years ago from the sex store. But I'm talking real flesh."

"Danielle, you're such a goof."

"I know. So does he have any hot brothers who would also have something equally hard?"

I paused then. "Actually, he does."

"Ooh, so are you thinking what I'm thinking?" she asked, and I just smiled to myself. I knew exactly what she was thinking, but I had no business trying to set her up when I didn't even really belong in this house myself.

Chapter 16

"So he does have at least one other really cute brother, and I actually think you would get along with him, but—"

"But what?"

"How are you going to show up here, Danielle? I'm a nanny. It's not like I'm a family friend who can invite someone over. This is a job."

"Well, I have an idea," she said. "What if I bump into you at a market or something?"

I groaned out loud. "What do you mean bumped into me at a market? What market?"

"I don't know, but we'll figure it out. The supermarket or something. Just make sure that you bring one of the family members with you, and I'll be like, 'Oh my gosh, Annie, I haven't seen you in so long. How are you?'"

I groaned. "You're not going to put on an Australian accent like that, are you?"

"Why? It doesn't sound believable?"

"I mean, it sounds believable, but are we really going to stretch this lie even further? My long-lost Australian best friend just showed up at the same random-ass market I did?"

"Fine, I'll be Scottish then," she said in a deep Scottish accent.

"That's not better, Danielle."

She giggled. "Fine. Maybe I'll just be regular old American me, and I'll say that I was checking out the town because you said it sounded so nice and just wanted to say hello to the family. Or rather, maybe I can be completely honest and say I wanted to make sure you were safe because I don't know anything about them. And it's a little weird that you're going to be living with people you don't know."

"That's what nannies and au pairs do all the time, Danielle."

"Yeah, well, you're special to me. We're best friends, and I'm going to check."

"But you're only checking because you want to meet Dylan."

"You're the one that said he's hot."

"I didn't use that word," I said.

119

"I know you're into Noah anyway." She laughed.

"I didn't say that. I—"

"Girl, if you weren't into Noah, you would've been begging me for a hundred dollars to get you a ticket to come home."

"No, I told you I'm staying because of the paycheck. And—"

"You hate kids."

"I don't hate kids. I love them so much. In fact —" I started laughing. "Okay. I mean, I can't say I love them, but I don't hate them."

"Girl, you said you didn't want to go to Disney because you didn't want to hang out with a bunch of kids."

"Because they cry, and they're annoying, and…" I paused. "Fine. Maybe I don't want to spend my whole day with them."

"But you realize that you just took a job where you're going to spend your entire day with kids."

"Not just kids," I said softly, "but bratty-ass kids." I groaned. "Okay, fine. Maybe a part of the reason I'm staying is because I'm intrigued by Noah St. James."

"Of course the money is amazing, but you want to see if the dick is good," she sang.

"Oh my gosh, Danielle."

"What? It's true."

"No, it's not."

"Yeah, it is. You just like big dick men."

"I've never even had a big dick man," I said, laughing.

"Ooh, don't let Donovan hear you say that," she said.

"I wish he would hear me saying it. I wish that —" I froze as I heard a loud noise.

"You there?" Danielle said.

"Yeah, I thought I just heard a noise."

"What noise? Oh my God. If that place is haunted, I'm not coming."

"I don't think it's haunted. I…" I paused again as the knocking on my door became louder. "I think there's someone at my door."

"Oh shit. Don't tell me it's the little kids coming to ask you to tell them a bedtime story or something."

"I don't think so. Lulu said I would start in the morning, so I wouldn't have anything to do tonight."

"Then who is it? Oh my gosh. What if it's Noah?"

"It's not Noah," I said as the knocking became louder. I licked my lips. "They're still knocking."

"Go and see who it is."

"Fine," I said. "Hold on." I kept the phone in my hand and made my way to the door and opened it slowly.

"I was beginning to think you were deaf." Noah stood there grinning at me.

"I'm not deaf. I'm on the phone with my best friend." I held it up.

"Okay. Tell her I said hi."

"Um, okay." I paused. "Do you want me to tell her now?"

"If you want," he said, chuckling as if I'd said something super hilarious.

I tried not to stare at his bare chest. It was the most masculine, splendid thing I'd ever seen in my life. He was muscular and tan with black hair covering his pecs. And it wasn't a gross gorilla sort of hair, but a light splattering of fine silky hairs that made me want to reach out and touch them.

"So are you going to tell her, or are we just going to stand here all night?" he said.

I rolled my eyes. "Hey, Danielle."

"So what's going on? Who are you talking to?" she asked.

"Noah St. James, my new boss, wanted me to tell you he said hi."

"Oh my God, he totally wants you," she squealed into the phone.

I batted my eyelids furiously, hoping he couldn't hear. "Well, I'll call you back in a little bit. I just want to see what my boss wants."

"Your boss wants to do you," she sang into the

phone. "He wants to make love to you. He wants to—"

"Bye," I said quickly and hung up. "Danielle says hello." I smiled at him. "And what can I do for you, Mr. St. James?"

"Mr. St. James?" He raised an eyebrow. "Since when do you call me Mr. St. James?"

"Well, since you said to me that—"

"I was just joking. Of course you're going to call me Noah. I mean, you're standing there in your pajamas, and I'm standing here in mine."

"Those are pajamas?" I said, staring down at his red silk boxers.

"You could say that," he said with a smirk. "To be quite honest, I don't sleep in anything."

"What do you mean you don't sleep in anything?"

"I sleep in the nude. But I figured as I was coming to say good night, I should put something on."

"You did that just for me?" I rolled my eyes.

"Would you have preferred to see me naked?"

"No, but I don't think your parents want to see you naked or Dylan or Lulu or the kids."

He started laughing then. "Touche," he said. "You're right. But I do sleep naked."

"But you don't wander down the corridors naked."

"No, I know," he said. "So am I going to be able to step into the room, or am I going to just stand outside the door like this?"

"I didn't know you were a vampire," I said, grinning at him.

He looked confused then and blinked. "Um, what are you talking about?"

"Well, vampires can't go into a place unless they're invited. You were asking me if I was going to invite you into the room, so I figured maybe—"

"I see," he said and stepped past me into the room.

"Hey, what are you doing?" I said quickly as he closed the door behind him.

"Well, I figured from what you were just saying that I could come in."

"I didn't say you could come in."

"But I'm not a vampire." He grinned. "So I don't need an invitation."

"Oh, you're so frustrating," I said.

"Am I?" He laughed. "Why? Are you upset I'm not a vampire?"

"Why would I be upset you're not a vampire?"

"Maybe you want me to sink my teeth into you."

"What?" I said, gawking at him.

"Maybe you want me to suck." He licked his lips and took a step toward me.

I stepped back. "Suck what? You want to suck my blood out or something?"

"No, that's not what I want to suck out," he said, winking at me.

I swallowed hard as I noticed that his eyes were on my chest. I could feel my nipples poking through my T-shirt. Fuck. Why hadn't I worn a bra? "Um, Noah, could you please tell me why you're in the room?"

"I think you know," he said softly. "I think you've been hoping this would happen all night long." And of course he was right. I had been hoping he'd come to my room, but now that he was actually here, I wasn't sure what to do next.

Chapter 17

"Noah, I think you're doing a lot of thinking about what you think I'm thinking, and it seems to me that everything you think I'm thinking is wrong."

"That sounded like a bit of a tongue twister," he said. "Was it hard to say?"

"No, it wasn't hard to say, but—"

"But what?" he said, taking another step toward me. I licked my lips nervously as he grabbed my hand and pulled me into him. "You know, there's just something about you."

"Yeah? What?"

"I don't know. There's just something that makes me want to do this," he said in a deep husky voice. I felt his lips pressed against mine. And even though my brain was screaming at me, telling me to push him away, I knew that I couldn't. I knew that I didn't want to. I reached up and ran my fingers through his hair as I kissed him back passionately. I gasped as I felt his hand reach up under my shirt and run up my back. His fingers trailed up and down my skin, teasing me in a line of passion that was fast building up in my body. His kiss intensified, and I felt his tongue slipping into my mouth, and I gasped as his right hand reached up and cupped my breast and his thumb rubbed gently against my nipple.

"Oh," I said against his lips, and he chuckled as he pulled away slightly. His fingers moved back down toward my stomach and ran across to my belly button. I bit down on my lower lip as his fingers then moved farther. I stared into his blue eyes, and I could see he was studying my face, waiting to see if I was going to stop him. But I couldn't. I didn't want to. I just wanted to enjoy tonight. I didn't care about anything else, and frankly, this was what I needed. This was what I needed to make me feel whole again. Fuck Donovan. Fuck every horrible, shitty thing that had ever happened to me. Tonight I was going to enjoy whatever happened.

His fingers slipped inside my shorts, and he growled when he realized I didn't have any panties on. "You were waiting for me, huh?" he said as his lips pressed against my neck, and all I could do was roll my eyes at him. He chuckled as if amused before kissing me again. I ran my fingers down his back and squeezed his shoulders. I cried out loud as his fingers slipped between my legs and rubbed me gently.

"Oh," I said, gasping as he caressed my most tender spot. I could feel myself growing wet, and I could hear the sound of the raspy growl in his throat as he realized how turned on I already was.

"Fuck. You are the sexiest thing. You know that, Taytum?"

I shook my head and gave him a small little smile as he ran his fingers back up and pulled my top off. He threw it to the ground, then pulled me toward him. His fingers ran up and down my back as my breasts crushed against his chest. We moved toward the bed and fell backward. I felt his lips against my throat licking down to my collarbone. His tongue trailed down to my nipple, and he licked and sucked. I cried out as he slipped his finger back between my shorts and rubbed me gently, then inserted not one but two fingers inside me.

"Oh," I almost screamed at my immense pleasure. It was so intense that I started giggling.

He frowned slightly and stopped what he was doing to look down into my face. "Why are you laughing?"

I could tell that he was disconcerted, that he'd

never had a reaction like this before. "I thought you were going to wait for me to beg," I said with a small little smile, loving the look he was giving me and how he made me feel. It was weird that I was so comfortable with this man when I hadn't even known him twenty-four hours previously, but I felt connected to him. I felt like he was destined to be in my life, and I wasn't going to argue with that feeling.

"I am," he said, chuckling as he reached down and pulled my shorts off. I lay on the bed naked, staring up at him. I watched as he pulled his boxers down and stared at his long hard cock as it stood to attention. My stomach felt like it had butterflies in it, and I knew he was the most beautiful man I'd ever seen in my life.

"Really?" I said. "Because from what I can see, I'm naked, and you're naked, and I haven't begged for anything yet."

"True," he said as he got back onto the bed and caressed me. He moved over on top of me and bent down and kissed my forehead. His right hand moved under my back and lifted me up slightly and spread my legs so that they were centered between his body. I felt him reach down and grab his cock and rub it gently against my opening. I gasped at the feel of his warm skin.

"Oh my," I said, my eyes fluttering back in my head. If Danielle knew what was happening now, she'd be screaming in happiness for me. She knew just how badly I needed something like this. She knew just how badly I needed a man to want me and take me because she wanted the same thing.

I giggled again, staring up at him.

"What is so funny, Taytum?"

"Just this whole situation," I said, grabbing his head and pulling him down to kiss him. He growled and kissed me back passionately, his fingers running up and down the side of my body as his cock rubbed up and down on my clit. "Oh yeah," I said, moaning, waiting for him to thrust inside me and for our bodies to become one. I needed it so badly. I wanted him. I was about to go crazy. "Noah," I moaned and then frowned as he started laughing.

"What's so funny?" I felt bereft as he rolled over and lay on the bed next to me. He stared at me with a cocky expression on his face.

"I think we should stop here."

"What?" I said, almost shouting.

"I told you. Nothing's going to happen unless you beg for it."

"But we... I..." I didn't know what to say. "You were just—"

"I was just having a little fun. But if you want that fun to become ecstasy, you're going to have to beg me, Taytum," he said, staring at my lips. His fingers reached over and played with my body, and I closed my eyes as I gripped the sheets. Every part of me wanted him, but I was not going to give in. I would not let him think he got the better of me.

A little birdie in my head was telling me to give up my pride. A little birdie in my head was telling me to beg him, to feel him inside me, to have an orgasm because I knew this man would not stop until I screamed his name in ecstasy. My eyes opened, and I looked over at him. I reached down and grabbed his cock with my index finger and thumb and moved it up and down.

"Or maybe you should beg me," I said with a sweet little smile. Two could play this game. Yes, I wanted him badly, but I wasn't going to act like a complete desperado.

Chapter 18

"SO IT APPEARS WE'RE AT AN IMPASSE," NOAH SAID AS we both lay there staring at each other. His hands were to himself, and my hands were no longer touching him. We were both staring at each other, lust in our eyes, desire in our hearts, yet neither wanted to beg the other.

"I guess we are," I said. "And I'm starting to feel cold, so…"

"So then you should cover yourself with the blanket," he said. And I watched as he sweetly pulled the blanket up and covered me.

"You didn't have to do that," I said, surprised at the action. I thought he'd say something like, 'Well put on some clothes,' or, 'get under the sheets,' or, 'I'll keep you warm if you beg me.'"

"Can I share the blanket with you?" he said, turning on his side and looking at me.

"Why would you want to do that?"

"Because maybe I'm cold as well."

"Fine," I said and held the blanket up.

He snuggled closer to me and smiled. "Thank you."

"You're welcome," I said. "You can also go back to your own room and snuggle under your own blanket."

"What fun would that be?"

"I don't know. Does it have to be fun?"

"It doesn't have to be fun, but I find that life is so much more enjoyable when it's fun, and you are someone who makes my life fun."

"Well, enjoy it while you can. I'm officially starting the job tomorrow, and I don't think those kids will give me much time or space to have fun with other people."

"So what did you think of my niece and nephews?"

I stared at him for a couple of seconds. There was a twinkle in his eyes. "I think they're great," I said, not quite truthfully.

"And you think you'll be the touch that they need?"

"Um, I'm a great nanny, but I'm not a miracle worker," I said, shrugging.

"Are you not? I thought you said on the phone that other families have called you a miracle worker."

"Um, what?" I licked my lower lip nervously. Had Annie really said that? Like what was she trying to do to me? Make me look like an idiot? I mean, not that she knew I was going to pretend to be her and take her job or anything. She'd probably been lying about her qualifications as well, and that's why she hadn't shown up. At least I told myself that to make me feel better.

"Hey, it's okay," Noah said lightly, touching my shoulder. "I know they're hellions, and they're wild. You'll do your best. And if your best is as good as they say, you'll have them under control in no time."

"I mean, I've only got one month with them," I said, making a face, "not one year."

"So you think you can fix them in one year, huh?"

"I'm not saying that. I'm just saying that it might take more than a month to get them under control. I have to figure out their base reasons for acting the way that they do and—"

"Why do kids scream and shout?" He shrugged. "Because they want to, right?"

"No," I said. "It's because they feel like they're

not being heard. So they want attention, and that's the only way they think they can get it."

"Interesting." He nodded. "I never thought about it like that."

"Yeah, well, you should. I mean, not that they're your kids, so it's not really your problem. But their mom, Lulu, she shouldn't spoil them. I feel that she's probably letting them get away with whatever they want to get away with because she feels guilty about something, but that's not helping them. She's just exacerbating the problem."

"Huh. You're very intuitive. I guess you really are the Mary Poppins of Manhattan."

"I guess so," I said, wondering where all that had come from. Maybe it was because I watched a lot of daytime TV and a lot of self-help shows. Anyway, I'll try my best. They're good kids, and I mean, I'm being paid a lot to help take care of them.

"I think they'll really like you. Maybe as much as I do," he said with a small smile.

"So you like me, do you?"

"I think I do. So, Taytum, tell me more about yourself."

"What do you want to know?"

"What do you do for fun? What did you see yourself doing with your life aside from being a nanny?"

"I like to draw and paint." Which was true.

"Oh, you mentioned something about art earlier."

"Yeah, it's my true passion. I love illustrating, especially children's books. In fact, one day, not anytime soon, of course, but one day, I want to write my own children's book and illustrate it and maybe make it a series. And I would love it if it became a cartoon, and I could work on those animations as well."

"You're really into art, huh? You must be very talented."

"I'm not bad," I said. "Obviously, I'm not the best, or I would be making an amazing living as an artist."

"But don't most artists only get recognized after they die?" he said, laughing.

I looked at him thoughtfully. "A lot of successful, really popular artists now weren't as recognized when they were alive. That's true. They weren't making as much money. I mean, certainly, their paintings weren't going for hundreds of millions like some of them are now. But many were recognized in their time and could make a living out of their art. I'm not."

"Maybe we could draw something one day," he said.

"Oh. You're interested in art?"

. . .

"*I* wouldn't go that far, but when I was in college, I did a semester abroad in Florence, and well, anytime you're in Florence, you learn a lot about the greats."

"Oh, I'd love to go to Florence," I said wistfully. "I've always told myself I'll go to Florence when I have enough money."

"Well, I guess you'll have enough money soon." He stared into my eyes, and I couldn't tell what he was thinking by the expression on his face.

"Yeah, that's true. Though I think I'll use that money for rent and bills and set up a little emergency fund for myself, you know?"

"Do you have another job lined up after Christmas?" he asked curiously.

I shook my head. "No, your generous paycheck will allow me to pursue my other love of art. So thank you."

"No, thank you. I'm sure it must have been hard to be away from your friends and family for Christmas to come and look after three kids you don't know, and three troublesome kids at that."

"Yeah, it was kind of hard. I mean, I think I told you before, my parents are going to the Caribbean, so it's not like I was going to see them, but my best friend."

"The one you were on the phone with?"

"Yes."

"You said her name was Danielle?"

"Yeah, Danielle. We were going to spend Christmas together. I guess I actually need to tell her that that's not going to happen anymore."

"Oh no, you didn't tell her about the job?" he said. "She doesn't know you aren't going to be in town?"

I just stared at him for a couple of seconds as I realized what I'd said. I'd almost outed myself, and I was nervous.

Chapter 19

"So I'm not sure that I understand exactly what you're saying." Noah frowned as he stared at me.

I felt his leg shift in the bed next to me, and I shivered slightly as his thighs pressed against mine.

"Oh, I just meant that even though my best friend, of course, knows that I have this job, I didn't tell her that I was going to be here for Christmas Day because normally we spend the season together."

I bit down on my lower lip. I didn't feel good lying. I didn't want to lie anymore, but I didn't know how to come clean. I felt like even though it had only been a few hours, I'd already gone too far down the path of deceit, and I didn't see how there was going to be any way to get back out.

"She actually was hoping she could come and spend Christmas with us," I said laughing, but I paused as I noticed that Noah's expression had changed slightly.

"I'm sorry. I didn't mean to bring that up."

"No, that just gave me an idea," he said, smiling suddenly.

"Oh, what's that?"

"Well, I've been feeling terribly guilty about the fact that we've taken you from your friends and family for the season. And yes, I know we're compensating you well, or rather I'm compensating you well, but money doesn't really make up for family and friends, does it?"

"It goes a long way," I said quickly, "and I'm appreciative. Of course, I want you to know that."

"I know you are," he said, nodding.

"But if your friend is interested and doesn't really have anywhere else to go, I know my parents and the rest of my family would be more than happy to have her join us."

"Oh, for Christmas Day? That would be lovely. Thank you." I nodded.

"No," he said. "For the entire month or for however long she wants to stay. I mean, you'll be busy working, and I'm not saying that you don't have to look after the kids, but maybe she can help you some days and maybe she can just explore the village. I don't know what she does for her job, but—"

"Wow!"

"You'd let your friend stay here as well?"

I stared at him incredulously. "Sure, why not?"

"But you don't even know me, and I know that you are a good person," he said, smiling warmly.

"Why do you say that?" I blink.

"Because I can feel it in my bones," he said.

"But we just met. Your bones don't know me well enough to feel anything."

"Let's just say I have good intuition. Why are you trying to tell me that you're not a good person?"

"No, I think I'm fairly decent, but I'm not perfect."

"And so you're saying you don't want your best friend Danielle to come?

"I'd love for her to come," I said, "but Noah!"

"Yes, Taytum."

"I'm your nanny. I can't have my friend coming to stay. It's not like I'm just here for fun. I'm here to work. I'm—"

"And I know you'll be serious and intentional about your job. I can tell just how much you care."

"What?" I said, my jaw dropping. "How?"

"The way you spoke up about how my sister is handling the kids. You were honest about your feelings that she was doing things you didn't think she should. And if you were just here for money, if you were just here to get by, you wouldn't have said anything. You would've pretended that everything was hunky-dory. You ever heard that saying, 'get in, get the money and get out'?"

"No," I said, shaking my head. "But I understand the principle."

"You care. Just like when you talk about illustrating children's books and writing your own book one day, I could tell that's something you're really passionate about." And passionate people, people with a purpose in their life, are good people. Those people strive for something more than just the want of money or power or even the want of love. Those people have higher goals and will do anything to get there."

"Wow! I feel like you're in my mind and heart and soul and spirit right now," I said, blinking at him.

"So there's something I want to say about you, Noah."

"Oh yeah. And what's that?"

"I think you have a shell."

"I have a shell?" He raised a single eyebrow.

"Oh no, don't tell me you think I'm some hard rich man who's broken by an ex or someone in my family and I can't love and—"

"No," I said, shaking my head.

"That's not what I was going to say at all."

"Then what were you going to say?"

"I was going to say, I think you have a shell because you're so rich, and you've probably been used before, and it may not even have been women, men use as well; lovers, friends, all sorts of people use. And I think your family is really important to you, and you want to make sure that they have the best and are taken care of and you would do anything to protect them and you love them. And one day, you do want to get married, and one day, you want a family as picture-perfect as the one you grew up in. I don't think you are hard or cold or cut off to relationships. I mean, I don't know you very well, but I don't get that vibe from you just because you're rich."

He nodded slowly. "You're very intuitive." He smiled. "I like that."

"I know you do," I said.

"And how do you know that I do?"

"Because of the look you're giving me, the warmness in your eyes. I like that look."

I wrinkled my nose. "I shouldn't say this, but my last boyfriend and I, we broke up very recently and I kind of thought we were going to get engaged this Christmas."

"Oh," he said, "it was serious then."

"No." I shook my head and laughed lightly.

. . .

"*I* know I should probably say it was serious if I thought we were going to get engaged, but I've been a bit of a fool. Actually, I was a lot of a fool, and that relationship was going nowhere for a long time, but I didn't want to acknowledge it. I think because I've had my head in the clouds for so many years, and I think I've always wanted something that just felt right, you know?"

He nodded, "I get it. A lot of times, we have a square, and we try so hard to fit it into a triangle piece. We'll even file down the square to make it fit, but it never quite does."

"Yeah," I said.

"Whoa, this is really deep, isn't it? For our first night." I started laughing.

"Well, it could be even deeper," he said, moving closer to me.

He wrapped his arms around me and pulled me against his chest. I stared at his lips for a couple of seconds. My heart was racing.

"Oh yeah. How is that?" I asked.

He turned slightly so that his hard cock was pressed against me.

And he grinned. "You just have to say three little words," he said, laughing. And I froze as I wondered if he meant what I thought he meant.

Chapter 20

"THREE LITTLE WORDS?" I STARED AT HIM, MY eyebrows raised, my heart beating furiously. He didn't expect me to tell him I loved him, did he? I mean, granted, we were moving really, really fast and anything was possible, but he seemed sane. I mean, at least saner than I was.

"Yeah, three little words," he said, grinning.

"So I'm not sure what three little words you're talking about right now," I said.

"Really?" he said, staring at me. "You can't think of what it is you need to say?"

He pressed his lips against mine for a couple of seconds, and I groaned as he reached down and lightly touched my stomach. I shifted slightly and he groaned loudly as my fingers brushed against his cock.

"What are you doing to me, Taytum?"

"I don't know. What are you doing to me, Noah?"

"Nothing yet, but I want to be," he said, his eyes firing shots of lust at me.

"Just say it, Taytum."

"Really? You're going to make me say it?"

"Yeah," he said, nodding.

I felt like I was officially crazy. I took a deep breath, grabbed his face, and pulled him toward my lips, then froze.

"What's going on?" he said.

"I just—"

"You just what?"

"I just can't believe you want me to say those words."

"I do," he said, nodding.

I felt his fingers on my ass, and I groaned slightly. I wanted to feel him inside me.

"Fine," I said, "I love you." I wrinkled my nose as soon as the words were out and shook my head. "I'm sorry. I shouldn't have said it. It's not even true. I'm sorry, Noah. You're hot, and I think you're funny, and I do like you, and I'd love to get to know you, but I don't love you. And—"

It was really weird because, in my fantasies, I would've wanted something like this, but it just feels really fast. I looked at his face and bit down on my lower lip. "I'm sorry. I just didn't think I would meet a guy who was hoping to go as fast as you are hoping to go and…" I paused as I stared at his lower lip twitching. "Are you laughing at me?"

He nodded slightly as if he felt bad. I watched as his lips trembled, and he started laughing out loud. "I'm sorry." He shook his head. "But did you just tell me you loved me?"

My eyes narrowed as I stared at his face.

"Because you told me to. You told me to say the three little words."

"I didn't tell you to say 'I love you.'" He grinned.

"Oh my! What three little words were you hoping I would say then?" I was so confused. What the hell was going on?

"I was hoping you would say 'put it in,'" he said, grinning at me.

"Put it in?" I stared back at him with wide eyes.

"Yeah, like put my cock inside your pussy."

*H*e winked at me, and I growled. "Put it in! Since when has anyone ever assumed that someone was going to know that they wanted them to say 'put it in' when they said 'say the three words'?"

He paused and nodded, but he didn't stop laughing.

"I guess you're correct."

"You guess?"

"I mean, you're correct." He grinned at me. "I just didn't expect that you would want me to fuck you so badly that you would tell me you loved me even though you don't really love me, which I think is a good thing because it would be really weird if you were in love with me and we just met earlier today."

"That's exactly what I was saying just now, Noah St. James." I glared at him.

"I've got a feeling I'm not getting any tonight. Huh?" he said, leaning forward and kissing me on the lips.

I didn't kiss him back this time. I was furious and embarrassed and a whole heap of other emotions that I couldn't even explain. I couldn't believe I'd been so desperate to feel him inside me that I told him I loved him and then taken it back. Then finding out that he hadn't even wanted me to say that in the first place was so cringey. I really was an idiot and needed my head examined. I was going to put some of the money he gave me aside so I could see a therapist because I had serious issues. I had to. Why did I keep making all these ridiculous mistakes?

"We can talk if you want," he said.

"I think we're done talking for the night, Noah," I said, shaking my head.

"Fair enough," he said, but he didn't shift. "So I have a question for you."

"Another question?" I paused. "Please do not ask me to say three words or two words or one word or five or ten or any, actually."

"Don't worry, I'm not going to. I mean, who knows what you'll say next?"

"Excuse me?" I said.

"I don't know. Maybe you'll be like, 'Yes, I'll marry you,' even though I didn't ask."

"Very funny, Noah." I rolled my eyes.

"Hey, I'm just saying. For all I know, tomorrow morning at breakfast, you'll be like, 'Hey, Pop Pop, I'm pregnant even though we never had sex."

I pressed my lips together. "That's not even funny, Noah."

"I thought it was a little bit funny." He grinned. "Maybe not funny enough to get me on late night TV, but definitely funny enough to get me in a comedy club."

"Maybe in a comedy club where they have tomatoes to throw in your face."

"You'd throw a tomato in my face if I said that joke?"

"If I had a tomato right now, it would be in your face."

He started laughing then. "This banter is amazing. It's so weird to actually feel like this."

"What are you talking about?" I was confused. "We're just having a regular conversation."

"I know, and I love it. I don't have regular conversations with women."

"What do you mean? What do you talk about?"

"They tell me about different sex positions they like, or different Tiffany's bracelets or trips they want to go on or hints about wanting to get married or hints about the fact they'd be down for a threesome or anal sex or the latest beads they bought."

"Oh, okay. Who are these women you're meeting?" I said, shaking my head.

"They sound like they're just trying to impress me and tell me what they think I want to hear," he said, "but I don't want any of that. I'm just a regular guy. I mean, a regular guy with a lot of money, but a regular guy at the end of the day."

"You are a bit of a bossy boots, and you're—"

"And I'm what?" he said.

"You can be infuriating and rude."

"And I told you that was a test."

"Was it a test when you were rude to me when I was talking with Dylan?"

He frowned then. "I don't know why you were flirting with my brother."

"I wasn't flirting with him. I was literally just talking to him."

. . .

"*U*h-huh."

"Anyway, I thought my friend Danielle might be interested in him, but oh, I wouldn't waste your time."

"Oh, why not?"

"Because Dylan, even though he doesn't know it, is dreadfully in love with his own best friend."

"Oh," I said, "do tell me more."

Chapter 21

"So your brother is in love with his best friend and doesn't know it?" I asked him. Now that he brought that up, I didn't need him to leave the bedroom so quickly.

Noah nodded. "I mean, my family and I have known that they've had a thing for years. Even though neither of them seems to acknowledge it or know it." He shrugged. "I don't know. They're both oblivious."

"So they've never dated?"

"Nope." He shook his head.

"Have they ever kissed?"

"Nope," he said. "They're best friends. They've been best friends since I can remember. I think they met in pre-K."

"Cool."

"Yet neither one of them has ever dated each other."

"They've never dated each other?"

"No, they haven't," he said, shaking his head.

"Then why do you think they're in love?"

"Because they're perfect for each other. And anytime she starts dating someone else, he tries to sabotage the relationship. And anytime he starts dating someone, she disappears and goes traveling around the world somewhere. Then inevitably, he dumps that person so he can go and meet her in said country. And that's been going on for quite a long time now."

"Oh wow. Crazy!"

"He'll go actually meet her."

"Oh really?"

"Yeah, she's in town. I think she gets in maybe tomorrow or the day after, and she will be spending time in the house with us."

"Oh cool."

"So if Danielle comes, I would tell her not to bother with Dylan."

"But you have two other brothers, right?" I said, grinning.

"That I do. They actually both should be here within the next couple of days."

"Oh cool."

"I think I told you one of them was on the train with you."

"Oh, yeah. Why didn't he get in the limo with us?"

"I really don't know," he said. "He's a little bit eclectic."

"Oh, in what ways?"

"You'll have to see when you meet him," he said. "If you think I'm a grump, then you will have to let me know what you think when you meet Ethan."

"Oh, I will definitely tell you how I feel."

"You're so pretty, you know that, Taytum?"

"Thank you," I said. "You're very handsome, and I'm sure you know that."

He smiled. "I've been told I'm a good-looking guy, sure enough, but that doesn't really mean anything to me. It's a compliment that doesn't hold much value when it's just told to you by random people. But when someone special, like you, tells me—"

"Oh, I'm special to you now?"

"Yeah. Do you really think I would've spent this much time talking to you if you weren't?"

I shrugged. "I don't know. I think you're just trying to get into my bed."

"But I'm already in your bed," he said, grinning, "and I've already got you naked. And if I'm quite honest, I already would've fucked you if I didn't think you were special."

"Excuse me!" I stared at him wide-eyed. "What does that mean?"

"It means that I would've rubbed my cock up and down on you for so long and so hard that you wouldn't have been able not to beg." He grins. "But I didn't want it to go down like that."

"*O*kay, so you still think that I—" He pressed a finger against my lips. "What are you doing?" I said.

"It's not fair to either one of us to pretend that we need the other to beg. I think it's quite obvious we both want each other."

I nodded slowly. "Well, you're the one who said I was going to have to beg you."

"Well, things change," he said. "Maybe we just do it when it comes naturally to us."

"Maybe we do," I said. "So what was it you wanted to ask me?" I ran my finger up and down his chest. "You said you had a question for me."

"Oh yeah. It's a little bit deep, and no, not my cock inside you, sort of deep, like real deep."

"Okay, well ask it."

"What do you think about death?"

"What do you mean?"

"Do you think that there's an afterlife? Do you think that people go to heaven and hell? Do you think that when someone dies, they're looking out for you like a guardian angel, or do you think that's it?"

I stared at him, surprised at the depth of his question. "I guess I never really thought about it before."

"Why?"

"A couple of years ago"—he ran his fingers through his hair—"a good buddy of mine, he died on a motorbike. He was going too fast. It was raining, and well, the semi didn't see him."

He looked in pain for a few seconds.

"He didn't make it. And sometimes I just wonder, you know, where is he? Is he looking down at me, laughing as I regale sentimental stories to you? Is he in the boardroom whispering in my ear, telling me to get more money? Is he protecting me when I go on helicopter rides, or is he just gone? We were supposed to go to Bali together. We wanted to go surfing, and I kept postponing the trip. I was too busy. I had deals to make, and I always regret not making the time, you know? And I wish I could just tell him sorry. I wish I could go back and take that trip with him, but I wish I could tell him not to get that motorcycle. I think he would've listened to me if I would've told him that I thought it was a bad idea, which I did, but I didn't want to impose my views on him, you know?"

He bit down on the side of his lower lip. "I don't even know why I'm talking about this with you. I don't even know why it came to my mind."

"It's okay. Maybe something in the past twenty-four hours has made you think about him, and that's why."

"Yeah, maybe. Or maybe you're just easy to talk to. I'm starting to realize how much I've missed having that."

"Having what?" I said softly.

"Having someone who listens, like really listens and isn't trying to cut me off and talk as I'm talking. Someone who cares. And I don't know, this is really fucking weird because we just met. But I feel like you're a kindred spirit. I feel like you're some sort of soul mate."

"I feel the same way," I said, nodding. "And it is kind of weird, but it's kind of cool."

"Yeah," he said, "it's the coolest thing ever."

Chapter 22

"I'm going to tell you my thoughts," I said after a minute or so. "I think when people die, when loved ones die, or people who we care tremendously about, I think they do visit us. I think they're our guardian angels and they protect us. When my grandma died a couple of years ago…" I paused as I thought about my nana. "I suddenly started seeing monarch butterflies. And it was weird because they would follow me around, and you just don't see butterflies everywhere, you know?"

He nodded. "And you thought it was your nana?"

"Yeah, anytime I see one, I say hi. You know, that's weird, but I feel like she's looking over me, protecting me. I mean, she can't stop me from doing stupid things because we have free will, but I feel like she's always there and trying to guide me. Sometimes I have dreams about her, you know?"

"Oh, yeah. What sort of dreams?"

"*I* had a dream where she gave me a locket, and she said, 'This is from your true love.'"

I smiled at him as I remembered the dream. "And it was weird because then she said, 'This is how you'll know he's the one.' And I always thought it was Donovan because, well, I guess maybe I wanted it to be him, but I always kind of knew that it wasn't. I even tried to hint to him that I wanted a locket for my birthday or for Christmas. But of course, he didn't get me that. But yeah, I know I'm rambling, but I think your best friend, Mikey…" He said that was his name, Mikey Johnson. "And I bet you Mikey is looking out for you, and he knows you cared, and he knows that you wish you would've taken that trip with him, but he doesn't blame you. He understands. He was your friend to the end, right?"

Noah nodded. "He was. I love that man like a brother." He sighed. You're a wise woman, Taytum."

"Thanks. I don't know how true that is, but I know what it's like to lose someone you love and not have in your life anymore. Sometimes I just want to call him, you know? I just want to be like, 'Hey buddy, want to get a drink?' Yeah, I want to call my grandma and say, 'You want to go catch a movie?' We always went to matinee movies on Saturdays. And there were some movies I took her to, she's like, 'Totally inappropriate,' but she just laughed all the way through. Then we'd grab something to eat, and she'd tell me about when she was younger and the dances she went to and all the beaus who wanted to date her and marry her. But she chose my granddad because he was the most handsome and smartest of them all." I smiled. "And he loved her. He died twenty years before her. But she said that she knew he loved her more than he loved apple pie. And he loved him some apple pie."

"Sounds like they had a really awesome love story."

"They did. She was my mom's mom, and I think that's why my parents have such an amazing marriage too, because my mom didn't settle for the wrong guy. And she and my dad, well, they were made for each other, but they decided to go to the Caribbean for Christmas." I nodded.

"It's weird, you know, some couples, they love each other so much that when they have children, they love their children to death and just constantly want it to be the family unit. And then other couples, they love each other so much that they only want it to be the two of them. I know my parents love me, and they love seeing me, but I'm not forefront in their mind, you know?"

He nodded. "I can say that my parents are the first sort of couple. They love us so much, and if they could have got us all to live in the same house for the rest of their lives, they would've been happy. And we all love each other a lot as well. I mean, we annoy the shit out of each other when we're together for too long, but I'm really lucky to have such a close family, and I do want that love one day, you know?

"I know I told you. I can see it in your eyes."

"Yeah," he said. "And you know what else you can see in my eyes?"

I stared into his eyes at the warmth reflected back at me, and I felt my heart flip. For a few seconds, I thought I saw love in his gaze, but there was no way in hell I would say that. Not after my "I love you" comment. And there was definitely no way that he was looking at me in love, looking at me with love. I mean, this wasn't the movies. People didn't fall in love at first sight. We hadn't even had sex yet, which actually made this evening even more special.

"I think I have to leave now," he said. "I should go to my own room."

I stared at him in disappointment. "Oh, okay."

"I don't want to go," he said.

"I don't want you to go either."

"I know, but I have a feeling Lulu will get the kids

to wake you up so you can give them breakfast. And the last thing we need is for them to see their naked Uncle Noah in bed with the new nanny."

I giggled slightly. "Especially seeing as we didn't even have sex, and everyone would assume that we had."

"Exactly," he said, laughing. Though if we had sex, maybe it wouldn't feel as bad." He winked at me.

"Is that your way of saying you want me?"

"You already know that I want you."

He pressed his lips against mine again, and I moaned. I reached over and pulled him on top of my body. His eyes looked into mine, and I nodded slightly. He pressed his lips against mine once again more forcefully, and his tongue slipped into my mouth. And I dug my fingers into his back. I spread my legs slightly and moaned as his fingers rubbed against my clit. I could feel my entire body shaking as he thrust two fingers inside me. And I closed my eyes and moaned as he made me feel things I'd never felt before in my life. He shifted and removed his fingers, and I felt the tip of his cock right there at my entrance. My eyes flew open. I could see he was staring into mine. His hands were brushing against my nipples. And I cried out. This time, we weren't playing games. And I felt him thrust inside me, and I couldn't stop. And I screamed.

Chapter 23

Noah chuckled and placed his hand against my mouth. "Shhh," he said, grinning, as he continued to thrust in and out of me. "We don't want to wake anyone up," he said, groaning.

I dug my fingernails into his back and nodded slightly. He moved his hand, and I cried out, moaning.

"Fuck! That sound is sexy," he said as he kissed the side of my neck and continued to thrust into me.

He started moving faster and faster, and I could feel my body bouncing up and down on the bed. My breasts slapped against his chest as he thrust into me harder and harder. I'd never felt such passion before in my life. I'd never felt someone inside me so deep and so hard, and I knew that this first time wouldn't last long. We'd been teasing each other for too long for either one of us to last.

He groaned as he pulled out of me and smiled as I stared up at him.

"Patience, dear Taytum," he said as he kissed me on the lips, then kissed down my body.

I closed my eyes as his tongue trailed toward my belly button. My entire body felt hot, and I shivered as I felt his hands on my thighs, spreading them wide open. His tongue moved farther down and suddenly was sucking on my clit. I moaned as I felt his tongue enter me, and I groaned and ran my fingers in his hair, pulling. He grunted before thrusting his tongue inside me. It felt almost as good as his cock, and as his lips sucked on my bud, I knew I was going to come within seconds. My body started bucking, and I couldn't control myself. I cried out and pressed my hand against my mouth to stop myself from screaming at the ecstasy coursing through my body. I exploded on his face, and he licked me up eagerly. I could hear him chuckling as he kissed his way back up.

"Look at me, Taytum," he said.

My eyes flew open, and he smiled. "You taste like strawberries and cream," he said, pressing his lips against mine.

I stared at him, not knowing what to say. I was slightly embarrassed but loving this moment with him. I wanted to say something back to him, but then he thrust into me once again and all thoughts of talking were gone. This time, he was moving harder and faster, and I could feel my body on the edge of a waterfall I didn't know existed. His thumb reached down and rubbed my clit, and I screamed out in passion. His eyes were clouded and dark, and he grunted as he thrusted harder, harder. He stilled then, and I felt him explode inside me until finally, he pulled out again.

He collapsed on the bed next to me, looked up at my face, and smiled. "Well, that was definitely a ten out of ten."

I smiled at him. "I think I'd give it a nine point five," I said.

He shook his head, laughter in his eyes. "Really?"

I nodded. "There's always room for improvement. I mean, that's odd. I always say this to all my students."

"Uh-huh," he said, grinning. "I don't want to leave," he said after a couple of minutes of us just laying there. My head was on his shoulder, and I nodded as I yawned.

"I don't want you to leave, either."

"But it'll be better," he said.

"I know." I nodded.

"It sucks that you're here to be the nanny, but I'm glad you are," he said, "or we never would've met."

"I know. It's kind of crazy to think that we just met this evening."

"I know. I guess it's a once-in-a-lifetime kind of thing."

"Is that what you tell all the girls, Noah St. James?"

"Just a few," he said with a wink. And I shook my head and hit him in the shoulder.

"That's not funny."

"What? Do you want me to tell you that you're special? That you are the only one I've had a night like this with?"

"*A*re you being sarcastic?" I said. Not sure how to feel about what he was saying.

"Not at all," he said, "I'm not going to lie. I've had sex on the first night I've met someone before, but have I had a real conversation? Have I felt like this?" He shook his head. "Not at all. This is special. This is real."

I beamed at him. "You make me feel amazing," I said, "and I think everything happened for a reason."

"You know what I really like about you, Taytum?"

"No. What?"

"I like that you're so honest and so beautiful and so wonderful."

"Oh, thank you." A part of me died inside at his words. Honest? How could I lie here and smile and act like everything was okay when one of the things he valued most about me wasn't true.

"And you know what, Annie Taytum?" he said.

I shook my head as he paused. I felt like he'd stabbed a knife into my heart when he said the word Annie. There was no Annie. I wasn't Annie. I had to tell him, but I didn't want him to hate me, and I didn't want to lose the job, and I just didn't know what to say.

"Let's not talk anymore. Just hold me for a while, and then I guess sneak back to your room. Or I guess you could go now if you don't want to wake up in a couple of hours."

"No, I want to hold you. We just made love for the first time. I don't want you to think I hit it and quit it." He chuckled slightly, and I rolled my eyes.

I ran my hands down his biceps. "You're so muscular."

"So I can protect you," he said.

"Protect me from what?"

"I don't know, uninvited vampires." He winked, and I giggled.

"You're a goof."

"Better than a grump."

"You're a goofy grump."

"I guess I'll take it," he said. "Come sleep for a

little bit. You've got a long day ahead of you tomorrow.

"You can say that again."

I closed my eyes and buried my face against his chest, breathing him in, not knowing if this would be the last time I had this opportunity.

"They're good kids. They just need some structure," he said against my head, and I nodded.

"They need a lot of structure, and they also need to lose their vocal cords." I froze as I realized what I had said, which obviously was a joke.

"It's fine," he said, chuckling. "I felt the same thing many times, but you are the expert. You'll get them to show their feelings and express their frustration and their want for attention in other ways, right?"

"Uh-huh," I said even though I had absolutely no idea how to do any of those things. And now not only was I feeling guilty about lying, but I was feeling guilty about the fact that the children weren't getting or going to get the adequate care and attention they needed. Me playing board games with them was not going to address the very real issues they had.

Chapter 24

A KNOCK ON THE DOOR WOKE ME UP THE NEXT morning, and I found myself stretching, feeling blissful. I looked over on the other side of the bed, but Noah was gone. I felt a little bit sad that he wasn't there and that I hadn't even realized he'd left, but it made sense. I wrapped the sheet around my body as the knock came again, and I walked toward the door, wondering if it was Noah bringing me a warning cup of coffee. I opened the door with a wide smile on my face. I could feel my face turning a bright red as I saw that it was Pollyanna standing there.

"Hi, Nanny."

"Oh, good morning, Pollyanna."

"Mommy said I should come and wake you up because I'm hungry, and so is Sammy and so is Theo."

"Oh, okay."

"And she said you'd make us breakfast and then take us to the park. And she said that, Oh, well, of course I just need to get ready. You should be up before us. All the Christmas nannies are always up before us," she said, pushing past me and walking into my bedroom.

S{he looked around. "I like this room." She went and sat down on my bed and looked at me with wide blue eyes.

"So do you want me to call you nanny, or should I call you Taytum or Annie or Mary Poppins II, or not good enough to be the real Mary Poppins or—"

I stared at her, and my jaw dropped at the words coming out of her mouth. How old was this kid? I walked over to her and stood next to her. I couldn't be rude. She was just a kid.

"So how old are you, Pollyanna?"

"I'm six. I'm the oldest. Sammy's next."

"And how old is Sammy?"

"He's four."

"Okay. And what about Theo?"

"Theo's five."

I frowned. "But you said Sammy was next."

"Yeah, he's my next favorite," she beamed. "Why? What did you think I meant?"

"Are you six or sixty, Pollyanna?" I said, laughing slightly.

"I'm six, but I'm soon going to be seven. I go to school. I'm in first grade, though Mommy says sometimes I act like I'm in twelfth grade, which is weird and silly because I've never even been to a high school. I don't even know anyone in high school. I like to play with my friends, and I love Barbies. I have fifty-two Barbies. Can you believe that? Fifty-two? I have more Barbies than anyone else I know. Pop Pop says that my Barbies need to have their own bedroom. And I said I would." She paused and rubbed her stomach. "I'm hungry. I want an omelet with bacon and cheese. Cheddar cheese, not—"

"One second," I said, holding my hand up. I was grateful that she wasn't screaming or shouting and the other kids weren't in here as well. But this was a lot. Let me take a quick shower, and then we..."

"You should have showered last night. It's faster. That's what the other nannies did because you have to wake up early to look after my brother and me then."

"Okay, I'll just put some clothes on real quick, okay?"

"Okay." She sat there staring at me.

"If you want to go and wait in the kitchen—"

"I'm okay. I'll stay here so you don't forget. And maybe I can have some Frosted Flakes. Mommy doesn't really like me to have Frosted Flakes in the morning because of the sugar, and she says we're hyper enough, but I love Frosted Flakes, don't you? Tony, the tiger goes roar."

"You know what, Pollyanna?" I said as I dug around in my suitcase for some appropriate clothes to wear.

"What?" she said.

"I can draw an awesome tiger. If you want, maybe today I can teach you to draw one."

"I'm not good at drawing," she said.

"Oh, but I'll teach you a couple of tricks. Maybe I'll give you some tips, and you'll be really happy with the drawing."

"Okay." She shrugged. "Are you going to be done soon because I'm hungry, Annie."

And before I knew what was happening, the two little boys had also run into the bedroom. Sammy and Theo stood there in just a T-shirt and shorts.

"Hungry, hungry, I'm really hungry," the one I think was Sammy started yelling. "Me too," Theo said, wrinkling his nose.

"Mommy says you should make his breakfast, Annie."

"Now, now, children," Noah's mom, Nana J, stopped by the door and smiled as I stood there brushing my hair quickly. Thank God I wasn't naked and had put on some clothes.

"Good morning, Taytum. I'm so sorry that the kids barged in on you like this."

"It's okay," I said with a small smile. Nothing was going to get me down today. Not after the absolutely amazing night I'd had last night.

"I was going to make breakfast for the kids. I love to make breakfast. But Lulu thinks you should make it so you can bond with them."

"Oh, of course. I don't mind making breakfast. I think we can have boiled eggs and toast. What does everyone think?"

"I want Frosted Flakes," Pollyanna said.

"I want sausages," Theo said.

"I want chocolate chip pancakes that look like Mickey Mouse," Sammy said. I stared at the three of them, my heart racing. What the…? I bit down on my lower lip.

And Noah's mom smiled. "Now, now, children, you can't expect Nanny Taytum to make all of those things, can you?"

"I guess not, Nana," Pollyanna said, "but it would be really nice."

"I know, but maybe today, seeing as she doesn't really know the kitchen, she can make boiled eggs and toast and maybe she'll make a menu for the rest of the week. Maybe you can help her make it."

"Ooh, I like making menus," Theo said. "I want chocolate pie and meatloaf."

"You just had meatloaf yesterday," Nana said.

"So can I ask you a question, please, Mrs. St. James?"

"Oh, feel free to call me Nana J."

"Oh okay, Nana J. Am I responsible for all their meals, breakfast, lunch, and dinner, or—"

Nana J smiled at me. "Well, I normally make dinner for the entire family. However, the kids sometimes like to eat earlier, so I think it would be best if you made breakfast and lunch and we can discuss the dinner plans. If it's something I can have made earlier, they could just have that. How does that sound?"

"Great, thank you."

"No worries," she beamed. "Now I'm off to putter around in the garden. If you need any help in the kitchen, the kids know where everything is."

"Okay, thank you."

"You're welcome. And I really am glad to have you here. We like to think that nannies are a part of the family, not just someone who works for us."

"Oh wow. Thank you."

"Now you all have a good day," Nana J said and walked out of the room.

"Are you nearly done yet, Taytum?" Pollyanna

said, crossing her hands over her waist. "I want breakfast, and I want to go into town because..."

"I want to go to the park," Sammy said.

"I want to go swimming at the beach," Theo said. "Mummy said that."

"Well, let's discuss that later," I said quickly, frowning. "First, let's get breakfast."

We all headed out of the corridor and toward the kitchen. I wondered if I was going to see Noah. It sucked that I was the nanny and not here as his girlfriend.

"Good morning, everyone," Dylan said, giving us a wave as we walked into the kitchen.

"Hi, morning Dylan."

"Hi, Uncle Dylan," the kids chorused.

I looked around to see if Noah was there, but unfortunately, he wasn't. So instead, I walked to the fridge and let out a huge sigh. This was going to be a long day.

Chapter 25

"So what exactly are the kids doing right now?" Isabella asked as we chatted on a three-way call with Danielle.

"They're swinging on the swings in the park," I said, sighing as I sat on the park bench. I'd only been with the kids for one morning, and it already felt like a lifetime had passed. "Thank God I have a moment of peace. I mean, they're lovely kids," I said quickly, just in case any of the moms in the park were listening to my conversation, "but they're just a lot of work."

"I bet," Danielle said. "So now that you've updated us on the nanny situation, what's going on with you and the hot men of the St. James family?"

"Well, I haven't met all the brothers, just Dylan, who's the third oldest. And he's cute, but I found out that he's probably in love with his childhood best friend or something."

"Oh, well, that sucks." Danielle sounded disappointed.

"But there are two other brothers, Ethan and..." I frowned as I struggled to remember the fourth brother's name. "To be quite frank, I forgot the other one's name," I said, laughing. "But they haven't made it home yet."

"Cool," Isabella said. "So what about you and Noah? What's going on?"

"So guys, you're not going to believe this." My face was hot just thinking about the previous evening. "I've been a bad, bad girl."

"Oh boy. What happened?" Danielle asked.

"We kind of hooked up last night."

"What?" They both shrieked into the phone.

"You did not hook up with a man you just met." Danielle sounded shocked. "You never hook up with guys you just meet."

"Well, technically that's true or used to be true, but Noah and I, we just have something special." I giggled. "I know that sounds crazy but—"

"Girl, last night you were literally saying he was a grumpy jackass."

"I did say he was hot, though."

"Yeah, you did say he was hot, but when I said

you only wanted to stay there because of him, you practically bit my head off."

"Yeah. Well, when he came to my room—"

"He seduced you," Isabella interrupted me and Danielle. "He had candles and whips and chains and—"

"Isabella, we're not in a BDSM novel, you know?"

"I know"—she giggled—"but how fun would it be to be a character in a BDSM novel?"

"I don't know if I'd want to," Danielle said. "I mean, it sounds like it would be kinky and fun, but I'm not here for the pain. Pleasure all the way, baby."

"Well, I heard a little bit of pain intensifies the pleasure," Isabella pointed out.

"You heard or you know?" Danielle asked. "Don't forget, we know you went to that sex dungeon a couple of years ago."

Isabella giggled. "Oh yeah. I forgot I told you girls about that."

"Are we talking about random-ass shit, or are we talking about the amazing sex I had last night?" I squealed into the phone. I looked around when I realized I was a little loud. "Hold on one sec. Let me make sure the kids are all still safe, okay?"

"Yes, Mommy," Danielle said, and Isabella laughed.

"Ha ha. Very funny, guys." I walked over to the swings. "You okay, Pollyanna?"

"Yes," she said, kicking her legs back and forth.

I then looked at Sammy and Theo, who also seemed to be having fun. "Are you two good?"

"We're going to go on the seesaw now," Sammy said, jumping off the seat and running.

"I don't want to go on the seesaw," Theo pouted.

"Well, I want to, and I need someone to go on the other side, and Pollyanna is swinging, and she's too big." He pointed at me. I tried not to feel affronted. I mean, I was too big, but was he trying to say I was too big because I was an adult or I was too big because he thought I was fat? I rolled my eyes.

"Well, guys, figure it out. I'm going to be right here."

"You're not supposed to be on the phone," Pollyanna said, giving me a look meant for someone far older than her.

"Sorry? What?" I blinked at her.

"You're being paid to look after us, and you're on the phone chatting away with your friends. And I—"

"Hey, girls, I might have to call you back in a second," I whispered into the phone.

"That little brat is not telling you you shouldn't be on the phone, is she?" Danielle said. "Oh my God, let me at her."

"Oh my gosh, Danielle, she's a kid."

"She sounds like a jackass."

"She's only six."

"Well, since when did six-year-olds act like jackasses?"

"I don't know, but maybe she's right. Maybe I shouldn't be on the phone on my first day of work."

"It's not even your job," Isabella said. "What are you going to do when the real Annie shows up?"

"Oh my gosh, girl," Danielle answered for me. "Taytum has the most ridiculous idea that will totally not work if the real Annie shows up."

"I don't think she's showing up. I mean, there's obviously a reason she wasn't on the train yesterday, and she hasn't called to let them know. I think I'm in the safe."

"You think you're in the safe?" Danielle said. "What does that even mean?"

"I mean I think I'm in the clear. Sorry. I'm watching the kids and I'm a little bit scattered right now. I'll call you back."

"Okay, but hurry. Did you see Noah this morning, by the way?" Danielle asked.

"No," I whispered quickly, which was something of a disappointment. "I haven't seen him since he disappeared from my bed last night, but I've got to go. I'll speak to you later." I hung up the phone quickly before they could ask me more questions because I knew what I wanted to do was chat with them about Noah St. James and not have to deal with these bratty kids. "Okay, guys, you've got five more minutes, then we're going to walk to the store because I need to pick up some stuff for lunch."

Pollyanna jumped off the swing. "I want to get a toy. I want to get—"

"Well, I don't know if you have any money to get anything," I said, smiling at her sweetly.

She crossed her arms in front of her chest and glared at me. "My uncle is one of the richest men in America. I can get whatever I want."

"Um, okay, but unless your uncle gave you money—"

Theo and Sammy were standing next to me all of a sudden. "Let's get ice cream," Theo said. "I want vanilla and chocolate and strawberry."

"I want rocky road," Sammy said. "Come on, let's go." The boys went running.

"Guys, we're going to the store where—" I screamed after them.

"You can't stop them when they want ice cream," Pollyanna said and went running after them. I found myself running after all three of them trying hard to keep up, but I wasn't in the best shape, and I wasn't used to running. This job sucked.

I soon realized I was not cut out to be a nanny, and I didn't care how much they got paid. This wasn't worth it. And it's not like they were my kids. I couldn't slap them or tell them no dinner if they didn't speak to me more politely. And it seemed like their mom didn't discipline them or even care. The next time I saw Noah, I was going to ask him just how much leeway I had with the kids. The thing was, I didn't want to get sued for treating the kids in a way that I shouldn't, and I knew that rich families were really sue happy. Imagine if I took away the kids' Oreo cookies or something, and next thing I knew, I got sued for emotional distress. That would suck. My hundred grand would be gone real fast then.

"Guys, hold on," I said, breathing heavily as I stopped next to them. "When I say stop, you must listen to me."

Pollyanna stared at me, blinking. "I didn't hear you say stop, Nanny Taytum." Theo and Sammy gave me angelic little smiles. "We were just running because you said we could go and get ice cream, and we wanted to make sure we got there before the store closed."

"It's one o'clock in the afternoon," I said, looking at my watch. "The store is not about to close. In fact, I didn't even say we could get ice cream. I said we were going to go to the store because I needed to pick up provisions to make you guys a late lunch, which will be sandwiches. Ham and cheese sandwiches with lettuce and mayo. And if you're lucky, you'll get some potato chips with that as well."

"I don't want a sandwich," Pollyanna said, shaking her head. "I want a Caesar salad with grilled chicken."

Sammy nodded. "And I want chicken nuggets. Dino chicken nuggets."

Theo looked at me thoughtfully. "And I want tomato soup with French bread."

My jaw dropped. These kids were really too much. "I have an idea," I said. "How about we have ham and cheese sandwiches for lunch, then I'll make burgers for dinner?"

"I love burgers," Sammy said as Theo grinned. They high-fived and jumped up and down in excitement. And I hoped that would exhaust them because I needed a nap after this little excursion.

Chapter 26

I WAS PHYSICALLY EXHAUSTED AND MENTALLY SPENT when I got back to the house with the kids. I had actually messed up because I'd taken them into a restaurant to buy them lunch instead of making them sandwiches because they've been bitching and moaning through every aisle in the grocery store. I knew that I sucked as a nanny, like absolutely sucked. And I wasn't sure how I was going to get through the rest of the week, let alone the rest of the month.

"Hi, Mommy," Pollyanna said, running into the house.

I watched as the two boys followed her, and I wondered how they still had so much energy when I felt like I could just collapse on the bed. My eyes lit up, though, when I saw Noah heading toward the front door.

"Hey, Taytum," he said, grinning at me widely.

"Hi, Mr. St. James," I said, winking at him. He smiled and shook his head, his eyes roving over my body.

"Hi, Uncle Noah," Sammy and Theo in unison.

"Hey, kids, were you good today?"

"Oh, we were really good, weren't we, Nanny Taytum?" Sammy turned to look at me, and I just nodded.

"They were children," I said, giving the most honest answer I could. Noah started laughing then. "So it was a long day, huh?"

"You could kind of say that." I nodded.

"Kids, run into the kitchen and go and hang out with Pop Pop and Nana J, okay?"

"Okay," they sang out and ran into the kitchen.

Walking up to me, he put his arm around me, pulled me into him, and gave me a long, hard kiss. "I missed you today."

"I missed you too. But what if someone sees," I said, pushing him away from me quickly.

"So what if they do?" he said.

"It's just not professional. Plus, I don't want them to think I'm easy."

"Why would they think you're easy?"

"Because I literally just met you yesterday, and we've already slept together!"

"True. We've also already had some really amazing conversations in the night as well."

"They were kind of cool, weren't they?" I said, beaming as I closed the door behind me.

"They were. So I was thinking that tonight you could sneak to my room."

"What?" I said, staring at him in shock.

"Well, I figured last night I stuck into yours, so tonight, you could sneak into mine."

"But what if the kids come to my room and—"

"Would you rather them catch me in bed with you in your room? Or them just not find you in your room. Plus, that way, you can spend the full night."

"You want me to spend the night?"

"Yeah. I was kind of disappointed when I woke up this morning, and you weren't by my side."

"Really?"

"Well, a little bit," he said. "I can't lie. I do enjoy my own space in the bed, but I wanted to see your pretty face. Then when I went for breakfast, you guys had already left."

"Yeah, the kids wanted to go to the park." I groaned as I thought about how that had gone.

"So I guess you're pulling out all your super Mary Poppin strengths, huh?"

"I guess so," I said, wrinkling my nose. "Right now, I want to pull out the trick where I can open an umbrella and fly."

"She flew?" he said, staring at me in surprise. "I must not remember that part of the movie."

"I might be making it up," I said, laughing. "I haven't seen it in a while."

"Me either," he said.

"In fact…" I wasn't sure why I was being so honest. "The only part of the movie I can really remember is when she sang that song, 'Supercalifrag-ilisticexpialidocious.'"

"Oh yes," he said, "I remember that song."

"You do?"

"You forget I have two nephews and a niece?"

"True, you do." I laughed.

He grinned at me. "Supercalifragilisticexpialido-cious. If you say it fast enough…" He started laugh-ing. "Well, I can't really remember the rest, but you know?"

"I know," I said. "So what did you do today?"

"Not much. I spoke to Ethan."

"Oh, the brother who hasn't made it yet?"

"Yeah." He nodded. "He's going to head over tomorrow."

"Oh awesome. I'm excited to meet him."

"And did you speak to your friend Danielle?"

"I spoke to her for a little bit but didn't really have much time."

"The offer still stands, you know? I spoke to my

mom and dad, and they would love to host more people."

"Oh, well, I didn't even mention it to her. I was actually on a three-way call with her and my other best friend, Isabella. And I wouldn't want Isabella to feel—"

"Invite her as well," he said, grinning.

"Two of my friends?" I stare at him in shock. "Are you hoping to have some sort of threesome or foursome or something?"

"No. Why would you say that?"

"I mean, it's just weird that you said I can have two of my friends come and stay when I'm just working here."

"I mean, are they nannies as well? Could they help you? Three kids, three nannies."

"It's not like they're going to work for free," I said. "I mean, I could always pay them part of my salary, seeing as you're paying me so much. But—"

"No, I would never want you to split the salary that I offered for just you, but I'm willing to pay them as well."

"Oh!" I said, my jaw dropping. "No, that's just way too much money."

"I don't mind if you'd be happy with more people here."

"No, I mean, I'll ask if they want to come, but

they're not nannies like me, so it wouldn't feel right for you to pay them. They'd just be happy to hang out. I'll ask them tonight."

"Why don't you ask them right now?"

"Oh, because I'm on the clock and working again."

"You deserve a break, Taytum. You don't have to work all day and night."

"Oh, thanks." I looked at him. "You're really different from what I thought you were going to be when I first met you."

"Oh, yeah?" And what did you think I was going to be when you first met me?"

"A super annoying grump," I said, laughing.

"And why is that?"

"*B*ecause you snapped at me, 'You are late!' Remember?"

"Well, you were late. I don't understand why you didn't take the first train. I don't understand why you didn't call us then."

"I lost the phone number," I bit down on my lower lip and lied. "That's why I wasn't able to call. That's why I was frazzled when I was getting off the train and looking around. But then John saw me and well, you know?"

"I'm glad we waited then."

"Me too," I said. "Thanks. And I was just a little discombobulated because, well, there was this guy on the train that was sitting in the carriage with me and he was really grumpy and mean, and well, I guess I was just in a weird mood."

"I understand," he said, "and you said you recently got out of a relationship?"

"Yeah, kind of."

"You kind of got out of the relationship or—?"

"No, I mean it was kind of a relationship. I don't think he thought we were official, but I kind of thought we were official." I sighed. "It was one of those things."

"I'm sorry. It must have hurt."

"It hurt. And I was embarrassed."

"And how long has it been since the relationship ended?"

I stared at him, not really wanting to tell the truth but not wanting to lie about this. I wanted our personal connection to be one hundred percent honest. "Yesterday," I squeaked out.

"Yesterday?" He raised an eyebrow. "Oh my. So am I a rebound?"

"No, of course not. I'm totally into you, and you have to know the sex was amazing. Like the most amazing sex I've ever had in my life. And—"

"Well, thank you," he said, "I would like to say

that the compliment is returned. So is he the reason you were late yesterday?"

I stared at him for a couple of seconds. "He is the reason I was on that train yesterday, yes." That was as honest as I could be right now. "But trust me when I say I never want to see him again."

Chapter 27

"So tell me exactly what happened yesterday," Noah said. There was a slight frown on his face as he stepped away from me.

"What do you mean? What do you want to know?"

"I have one question for you, Taytum."

I swallowed hard. "Okay, sure, go ahead." This was it. He was going to ask if I was Annie or not.

"If your boyfriend or semi boyfriend or whatever you want to call him, and you had not broken up yesterday..."

"Yeah?" I said, swallowing hard.

"Would you still have taken this job?"

I stared at him with wide eyes. "Wait, what?"

"I want to know, would you have still committed

to this job if you and your boyfriend hadn't broken up?"

I searched his face, looking to see if he was jealous, but he had a look of contrition on his face as if he felt like he'd made a mistake with me, like I was a bad person or something. "Are you mad at me?" I blinked at him.

"I just think when someone accepts a position as a Christmas nanny for a family and knows that it's a very important position and that a family is relying on you, that one should always fulfill their obligations, whether or not something else comes up, for example, a relationship working out when you thought it wouldn't."

My jaw dropped. "Are you saying that you're mad because you think if my relationship would've worked out, I wouldn't have come?"

"That's exactly what I'm saying."

"And that upsets you because you are jealous that we wouldn't have been together or—" His eyes narrowed.

"No. It upsets me because as a businessman—"

"So all of a sudden, this is about a business relationship and not about you and me, and what happened last night."

"What happened last night was personal. It was fun," he said. "I enjoyed it, and you enjoyed it, but you are not here because of that. You're here because—"

"Yeah," I said bitterly. "I'm here to be a nanny to three kids, and that's always first and foremost on my mind. Don't worry about it."

"I'm not worried about it. I just…you didn't say that you and your boyfriend just broke up yesterday. I mean, what was I, rebound sex?" Were you even telling the truth when you said I was the best sex you ever had, or was I just the best sex you had this week?"

My jaw dropped. "Excuse me?"

"I'm guessing you and your boyfriend had sex recently."

"Actually, we haven't. Not that it's any of your business."

"Oh, so you guys didn't have a quickie yesterday before it ended, and he decided to catch the next train?"

"No, that's not what happened at all. He didn't even know I was going to be catching the train. He —" I stopped. I couldn't really say much else because if I did, he'd want to know more information and then the full truth would come out, and I couldn't afford to let that happen. If he was this upset about something as minute as this, imagine how he'd feel if he knew about my true lie. I touched his shoulder. "I should have told you." I nodded.

"I realize that. But I mean, how'd you lie in bed with someone butt naked and ask them to fuck you, then in the next breath say, Oh, my boyfriend and I broke up a few hours ago?"

"A few hours ago?" He blinked. "So it wasn't even in the morning?" He shook his head.

"So you're telling me that literally hours before we hooked up, there was a possibility you were going to hook up with another man?" I bit down on my lower lip. He wasn't lying, of course. I mean, if Donovan had been excited about me joining, and if for some reason his parents had let us sleep in the same room, and if Donovan was up for it, we may have had sex. It wouldn't have been good sex. I probably wouldn't have come one or two or three times like I had with Noah, and I wouldn't have gone down on him, and I certainly wouldn't have swallowed. But I didn't want to go into all that information with Noah. I sighed. "I don't know what would've happened if things had worked out."

"So exactly what happened," he said.

"He was cheating on me"—I shrugged—"with this bitch." I paused as Noah raised a single eyebrow.

"So yeah, I can tell you're really over it."

"No, I am. I mean, of course I was shocked and hurt, but he really wasn't the man for me. Not at all. In fact, I was thinking of breaking up with him anyway, so that's why I was able to move on so quickly, you know?

I knew the white lie wasn't true, but how could I tell him 'I thought that perhaps Donovan was going to propose to me and I'd be a fiancée this Christmas'? There was no way in hell Noah would like to hear that.

"Okay," he said, "so it was a mutual breakup. You were going to break up with him whether or not he was cheating on you?"

"Yeah," I said, "totally. I'm going to be completely honest here, Noah. Sex with you was mind blowing and amazing. And I'm not lying when I said I've never had an orgasm like that before in my life."

"You mean several orgasms like that?" he said with a wicked grin.

I laughed. "Several! In fact, sex with Donovan wasn't even good." I lick my lips nervously. "So I don't regret anything about last night, and I hope you don't either."

"I don't," he said. "In fact, I wouldn't mind a repeat right now."

My eyes widened in shock as he ran his fingers across my breasts. "Oh my gosh! You can't do that. Anyone could see."

"Like I told you, does it matter?" he said.

"Yes, I just got here yesterday. And I don't want your parents or your niece or nephews or your sister to think I'm some sort of ho. I mean, yes, I did love the movie *Pretty Woman*. And yes, I was so happy when they got together at the end. And yes, I would like a love story like that myself. But no, I don't want to have to walk the streets to find my perfect partner."

Noah's lips were trembling, and I stared at him through narrowed eyes. "What's so funny?"

"You are," he said, shaking his head. "You say the craziest and weirdest things, but it's cute."

"I'm sorry. I like to mumble and ramble and… my best friend, Danielle, thinks I live my life in a romance book or movie. And I really don't. I mean, I love romance books, and I love romance movies, and Hallmark Christmas movies are my absolute favorite. But it's not like I think they're real life. It's not like—"

"It's okay, Taytum," he said, kissing me on the lips. "I like you. And that includes all your odd little eccentricities."

"You think I'm eccentric?" I pouted, not finding it much of a compliment, but then started laughing as he kissed my nose.

"You're very eccentric, but I like quirky. I like real. Now. You better head to the kitchen before my sister wonders where you are."

"Yeah," I said, smiling. "Let me go and take care of the——" I paused before I said hellions. He laughed then.

"And tonight you'll come to my room?"

"Okay," I said with a nod. "I will."

Chapter 28

"I'LL HUFF, AND I'LL PUFF, AND I'LL BLOW YOUR house down," I said softly and smiled when I realized Sam and Theo were finally asleep.

I closed the book softly and stood up and headed toward the door. I was surprised to see Noah standing in the doorway smiling at me with an odd look on his face. "Hey," I said, "I didn't see you there."

"I know. I was just enjoying your storytelling," he said softly.

"You could have come in and said good night to the boys."

"Oh, I would've just gotten them riled up." He shook his head. "And I know when you can get them to sleep, it's a good thing."

I smiled. "Yeah."

"I can't believe this is just day one. Are you over-whelmed?" he said, staring at me.

"No! Why would you say that?"

"I know they're a lot. They've been through a lot, and their mom is not very strict. I guess, neither are myself or my brothers. My parents don't like to intervene. They need structure. They need someone they can rely upon."

"Do they have a nanny during the year as well?"

He shook his head. "Lulu thinks she can handle them herself. She doesn't want to be one of those parents who isn't the sole caregiver." He shrugged.

"I understand, but she doesn't do the best job. She's super sweet, though."

"She is. I love her. She's my baby sister."

"So would you like something to drink? A night-cap, perhaps?"

Oh, I would love one, but I looked at my watch. "I promised Danielle and Isabella I'd give them a call, and I wanted to do that before it got too late."

"Okay." He nodded. "So how about we say in an hour?"

I blinked. "An hour for what?" I lick my lips nervously.

"For you to come to my room and let me ravish you," he said, chuckling slightly. "No, meet me in the study in an hour. We can have a drink and talk and see where the night takes us."

I smiled at him. "Is that your way of saying, see where the night takes us…aka to a night of passion and making love?"

"No." He shook his head. "If that was my way of saying that, I would've said, 'let's just fuck.'"

My eyes widened at his crude words, and he started laughing.

" I'm joking of course. Unless he prefers me to say that."

"Not really. Why would you ask that?"

"I know some women like dirty talk."

"Dirty talk?"

"Yeah, you know?" he said, his lips getting closer to my ear.

"No." I swallow hard. "What do you mean?"

"You know, something like, 'I want to fuck you so badly right now. I hope your panties are wet.'" He blew into my ear, and I trembled slightly. "I want my cock inside your—" I gasped as I saw Pop Pop coming down the corridor.

Noah turned and saw his dad. "Hey, Dad!"

"Hey, Noah! Taytum! What are you two up to?"

I wondered if his dad could see that my face was bright red. I wondered if his dad could tell that my entire body was tingling with anticipation for what would happen later that night. I wondered if he could read my mind and hear how my brain was telling me that maybe I did like dirty talk. No man had ever talked to me dirty like that before, and I never would've thought I'd enjoy it. But he turned me on in thirty seconds with just his words. He hadn't even touched me.

"Well, Taytum's going to call her friends, and I'm just going to have a nightcap," Noah said to his dad.

"Care for a whiskey?"

"Oh wow," Pop Pop said. "I mean, I guess I could have just a small shot," he said. "Don't tell your mom. I told her I wouldn't drink anything until Christmas."

"Oh, Dad," Noah said, laughing, "and she believed you."

"You know your mom. She knows me well enough to know that when I say I won't drink till Christmas, it just means I won't have several drinks."

Pop Pop smiled at me. "How did your first day go, Taytum? It seems like you and the kids got along well."

"Yeah, it was great. They're wonderful. So loving."

"I know they're a handful." He smiled. "But they really are good children. They just need some consistency in their life."

"Sure, I can understand that." I smiled. "Well, I'm going to head off to my room and call my friends—"

"Oh, and Taytum," Noah said as I headed toward my room.

"Yeah?" I asked him curiously.

"Don't forget the offer still stands. Your friends, Danielle and Isabella, if they want to come up, they're more than welcome here. I already spoke to Dad and Mom, and they're more than excited to welcome them."

"Yes, dear. Feel free to have them over. I know that you're here for a job, and I know you might be concerned that we'll think you're overstepping the bounds, but it's the Christmas season. The more people, the merrier." Pop Pop smiled, and I beamed at him.

"Thanks. I'll mention it to them now. Have a good evening, everyone."

"Good night, Taytum," Noah said. "Sweet dreams."

"You too," I said, blushing slightly and heading to my room quickly. As soon as I reached my room, I pulled out my phone and called Danielle.

"Hey, girl. What's up? Hold on, let me add Isabella," I said and placed her on hold to do a three-way call.

"Hey, what's up?" Isabella said.

"Not much. Danielle, you there?"

"Yeah, I'm here."

"Isabella, you there?" I said.

"I'm here."

"Hey, Danielle. Hey, Isabella. Okay," I said as I sank down onto the mattress, "guys, things are getting crazy."

"Like how?" Danielle asked.

"Like Noah wants me to come to his room tonight."

"How is that crazy?" Isabella said, "You guys just banged last night."

"We made love, Isabella."

"Same difference. You just met him. It's not love. It's banging."

"You're so crude."

"I know," she said, laughing, "but I call a spade a spade."

"Oh! And Danielle, I spoke to Noah and he said that you're more than welcome to come and stay. You too, Isabella."

"What?" Isabella sounded shocked. "Staying in the house with you?"

"Yeah. I guess they feel bad that I'm not going to be with my friends and family for Christmas. And I guess I kind of said that I'll miss you guys. And they said you're both welcome."

"Sweet," Isabella said. "So what, we come up on Christmas Day or something?"

"No. You guys can come up as soon as you want. You can stay as long as I'm here."

"Oh yeah," Danielle said, "I'm down for that. They're providing the food, right?"

"I guess so. But we can't eat them out of house and home," I said, groaning as I realized I repeated the words that my parents always said to me. "But they have plenty of food, so I'm sure you won't."

"Okay, I'm coming up tomorrow," Danielle said. "Can you pick me up at the train station?"

"I'm sure I could figure out a way or at least get a cab."

"I can make it tomorrow too," Isabelle said. "This is going to be so much fun."

"Yeah, I think it will be. But you guys, you have to remember one thing."

"Yeah, what is it?" Danielle asked.

"I'm a nanny, and I've been nannying for over ten years… and well, my real name is Annie Taytum and—"

"Oh Lord, we have to lie as well." Danielle sighed.

"If you want to come, we have to stick to the plan."

Chapter 29

"I have something special for you, Taytum." Noah walked over to me with a cup in his hand, and I stared at him with a curious expression on my face.

"Oh, what is it?" I took the cup from him gingerly.

"Ah, take a sip and see."

"Okay." I brought the cup up to my mouth and took a sip. I moaned as I realized what he'd given me. "Eggnog with rum. Wow! Thank you. It's delicious." The delicious creamy concoction slipped down my throat smoothly.

"I'm glad you approve." He nodded and held his own cup up. "I have the same myself."

"You're so sweet. I didn't even know there was eggnog in the fridge. I didn't see it."

"I got some today while you were out. I wanted to make sure you had something you enjoyed."

"Oh, thank you. That was really thoughtful of you."

"You'll find I can be a thoughtful man sometimes when I'm not being a grump or a bore."

"I never said you were a bore." I laughed.

"But you did say I was a grump."

"Because you can be a bit of a grump sometimes."

"Well, you ain't seen nothing yet," he said, laughing. "My brother Ethan is the grumpiest of us all."

"When is he going to be here?" I asked him curiously. I'd heard so much about Ethan, yet I still hadn't seen him.

"I think Mom said he'll be here tomorrow."

"Oh, cool."

"Yeah. I think you'll get along. Hopefully not too much."

"Why? Is he interested in his best friend as well?"

"No." He shook his head. "He's just really about his work right now."

"Oh, what does he do?"

"He's a professor of history at Cornell University in Ithaca."

"Oh, wow." I nodded. "Impressive."

"Yeah, his students hate him"—he chuckled —"and he loves it."

"Oh boy. Why do they hate him?"

"Because he's hard, which I... I'm not surprised about, but I don't want to talk about my brother right now." He looked around the room, then kissed me on the cheek. "Why don't we talk about something more fun?"

"And what do you consider to be more fun?" I said.

"Well, I don't know. You and me in bed doing the—"

I started laughing then, and he paused. "What's so funny?"

"Just you are," I said, shaking my head as I took another sip of my eggnog. "Oh. And I spoke to Danielle and Isabella, and they're both really excited to come. They're going to try to see if they can make it tomorrow."

"Awesome, he said.

"They're going to let me know what time the train tickets are for, and if I can't pick them up, maybe you can, or—"

"We'll figure something out." He nodded. "We'll have a full house. My mom will be ecstatic."

"Yeah. I hope she will be." I made a face. "I should have asked her before I invited them."

"No, I already told you it's okay. Don't worry so much, Taytum."

"I know. I just don't want to put more on her plate."

"Trust me. You've taken off the biggest troubles on her plate." He laughed. "She loves her grandkids, but they're a handful, even for someone who's raised four kids herself."

"Yeah, those three really are a handful," I said, nodding. "But let's not talk about the kids right now. Let's talk about something more enjoyable."

"Ah, so you want to talk about it as well?"

"About what?" I said.

"My cock." He winked at me, and I rolled my eyes.

"That's not what I was going to say."

"Oh, really?" He laughed. "So you don't find my cock enjoyable, then?"

"I didn't say that. I just… Why do you keep saying that word?"

"Maybe because I like the way your eyes go all wide and you blush when I say it."

"Are you trying to shock me?"

"I think I'd have to do a lot more than say the word cock to shock you, Taytum."

"Well, maybe," I said. "Shall we sit?" I looked around, and we moved toward one of the couches.

"Indeed. Let's sit," he said. "Are you enjoying

your drink?"

"I love it. Thank you."

"Would you like some cookies or something?"

I did want a cookie, but I didn't want him to know I wanted a cookie. I didn't want to look too greedy. "I'm okay for now, but thank you." We sat on the plush velvet chair, and I looked around the room. "It's so cozy in here. I love all the little decorations, the elves on the shelves." I looked at the mantelpiece over the fireplace. "The Christmas tree, all the tinsel." Above the door, I saw some mistletoe. "And look, there's even mistletoe."

"There is." He nodded. "And you know what mistletoe means, right?"

"What?" I laughed, though of course I knew.

"Every time you see mistletoe, you have to kiss." He leaned forward and gave me a kiss on the lips, and I kissed him back passionately before pulling back.

"That's actually not what it means." I grinned. "If you're standing under mistletoe, then you have to kiss. Not if you just see it."

"That's not as fun." He laughed.

"What do you mean?"

"I mean, how often do you find yourself under the mistletoe? I think it should be if you see mistletoe, you kiss the person you're with."

"You just want to kiss me," I said.

"I do like kissing you, but I don't need an excuse of mistletoe to do that."

"We have to be careful, though, because if someone sees us, I—"

"You what?"

"I just don't want them to think that… Well, I don't know. It just seems weird that I just arrived here as a nanny, and I'm already hooking up with you."

"But it's more than just hooking up, Taytum. We're getting to know each other where—"

"You have to admit that it's an odd circumstance, though."

"I suppose." He shrugged. "But there have been odder circumstances. Did you ever hear how my parents met?"

"No. Don't tell me. Your mom was a Christmas nanny, and your dad was—"

"No." He cut me off, laughing. "That was not how they met."

"So then how did they meet?"

"Maybe I'll wait to tell you," he said. "Maybe I'll have them tell you. They will make it sound a lot more fun than my retelling."

"Oh, but now I want to know."

"You'll know soon enough. And I'd rather we talk about ourselves." His hand moved down to my leg, and I felt him running his fingers up and down. I reached over and placed my hand on the side of his face and kissed him on the lips. He kissed me back passionately, his tongue slipping into my mouth, and I moaned against him. I felt his chest hit my hand, and a bit of the eggnog spilled, and I pulled back. "Oops," I said. "Sorry." I touched the wet spot on his shirt, and he just laughed.

"It's okay. I don't mind. If you want to lick off the drops, you can."

"I'm not going to lick off the drops," I said, laughing, then I lowered my voice. "I mean, maybe if it was on your skin I'd lick it off, but it's on your shirt. I don't know where your shirt has been."

"Oh. So you want to lick something off my skin tonight, do you?"

"I didn't say that. I—"

"There's whipped cream in the fridge."

"Is there now?" I stared at him.

"Yeah. My mom got it for ice cream sundaes for the kids. But we can use it tonight, and I'll run out and get more tomorrow."

"Noah, we cannot steal the whipped cream just so we can—"

"Just so we can do what?" He winked at me. "I don't know what you're thinking, but spray it on each other's bodies and lick it off. You're telling me that doesn't sound delicious?" he said.

"Fine." I giggled. "Let's do it. Let's do it now."

Chapter 30

"So here's one can of whipped cream, some chocolate syrup, and some maraschino cherries." Noah held up the goodies in his hands and grinned at me.

"Oh my gosh. What are we going to do with all those?"

"We can have human sundaes," he said, licking his lips.

"I know some spots that I would like to lick clean off you."

"Noah." I laughed. "Really?"

"What?"

"I mean, that just sounded weird."

"You're calling me weird, Mrs. Rambling about all sorts of crap all the time?"

"I don't ramble. I just… Okay, fine, I ramble. But

it's because I am a creative type. I like to draw and I like to write. And—"

"I know," he said. "So what got you into working with kids?"

"Um, circumstance," I said quickly.

"Do you think you want to have a large family of your own one day?"

I stared at him for a couple of seconds, not sure how to answer that. "I mean, sure. I've never really thought about it. I mean, depending on what my husband wants, I'd like to have some kids for sure. I wouldn't say that—" I paused as I bit down on my lower lip.

"You wouldn't say that what?" he said.

"I wouldn't say that I wanted a basketball team or anything. Kids are hard to handle."

"Yes, they are. But when you have a partner who's hands-on as well, it's not so bad."

"Yeah, true. So do you want to have a lot of kids?"

He grinned. "I'm thinking about seven."

"Seven?" My jaw dropped. "Say what?"

"Well, maybe I'll have five If my wife is not down for seven."

"Five? That's still a lot." I shook my head.

"Well, I take it you don't want to have five kids then, huh?"

"Um, like I said, I've never really thought about

it, but I certainly haven't had that number in my mind."

"So what's the most kids that you would have?" he asked me curiously.

"I don't know, like three. Three kids can fit in the back of the car and the parents are in the front."

"Yeah, but they make bigger cars now. There are cars that have three and four rows, and there are minivans."

I wrinkled my nose. "I don't see myself as a minivan mom. I mean, I don't live in the suburbs, and I don't really expect to live in the suburbs."

"Oh. You want to live in New York your entire life, even when you get married and have kids?"

I stared at him for a couple of seconds. "Um, I haven't really thought about it. I haven't lived in New York that long, and I haven't really lived, you know, the New York City life of my dreams."

"And what's the New York City life of your dreams?" he said.

"You'll just laugh at me."

"I promise, I won't. What is it?"

"I thought we were supposed to be having sexy time right now." I nodded toward the whipped cream and cherries.

"We can have sexy time whenever. I like talking to you. I like getting to know you."

"Okay. Well, the New York City life of my

dreams is me shopping for fashionable clothes and going out to restaurants and gallery openings, and hobnobbing with the rich and famous and beautiful. And getting to meet really esteemed artists and being invited to my own gallery openings and making a name for myself and having people want to come to my shows and buy my art. Then meeting the man of my dreams and traveling the world, going to Greece and Italy and France and Kenya and South Africa and Brazil and even Antarctica."

"So you like to travel?"

"I do. I haven't gotten to travel much recently, but that's because of finances." I wrinkled my nose. "I do see myself getting married and having a wonderful family and a loving husband. And maybe after that, moving Upstate to a nice traditional farm-house and having a couple of chickens and a cow to get fresh milk, and some goats and an herb garden. You know? The picture-perfect life."

"I can see you've thought about it."

"I have. I mean, half of it is based on Hallmark movies, but it's what I want for myself too."

I don't know if that sort of life actually exists, but if that's what you want, that's what you should be able to have. And your ex, this Donovan, he would have been able to provide that for you?"

I stared at him for a couple of seconds and sighed. "I don't know."

"You don't know? Then why were you with him?"

"I had this idea of who he was and who I was when I was with him and who we were as a couple and where we were going, but I was trying to force it. My friend Danielle says it was like trying to force a square puzzle piece into a triangle. It didn't quite fit. And the more you tried to push it in, the more you damaged the square piece."

"So you damaged yourself trying to be with him?"

"I wouldn't say I damaged myself so much as I kind of made myself look like an idiot and a fool."

"Because you were in love with him?" he asked. There was a light in his eyes that told me that question was really important to him.

"No." I shook my head. "I wasn't in love with him, and he wasn't in love with me. And we never told each other that we were in love. I just guess I wanted the relationship to be more. I figured if we got to spend more time together and I met his family and we did all the things that I thought you were supposed to do, then it would just work out."

"I see," he said.

"What about you, Noah? When was your last relationship?"

"About a year ago."

"And was it serious? Were you engaged or—"

"We weren't engaged, but it was fairly serious, I suppose."

"Okay." I nodded, though I could feel a surge of jealousy coursing through me. I didn't like hearing that.

"She was a nurse," he said. "I met her through a friend of mine. She was his little sister, and we had a lot in common. She was smart and witty, and she understood that I didn't have a lot of time. She was actually a travel nurse, so we didn't see each other that frequently."

"And what happened?" I said.

"She took a job in Seattle, which was fine. I didn't really mind. When I would fly to the West Coast, she would come and try to see me and she would fly back to New York every now and then."

"Okay. And what happened?"

"It just kind of fizzled," he said. "I went to San Francisco on a business trip and she messaged me a week later asking how I was doing. And I said, 'Good, what about you?' And she said she had just moved to San Francisco. I said, 'Wow, that's amazing. I was just there last week.' And she said, 'But you didn't even let me know you were going to be on the West Coast.' And that's when we kind of both knew that we weren't really important to each other. We were just having fun."

"I see," I said. I didn't want to think about him

with another woman. "And so then what happened?"

"So then we got off the phone, and we haven't spoken since." He shrugged. "I mean, it wasn't anything serious, and I haven't even thought to call her and she hasn't called me."

"So it was just a sex thing?"

He shook his head. "No, it wasn't just a sex thing, but it wasn't more than that, if that makes sense."

"It does," I said. "I guess."

Chapter 31

"Don't be jealous, Taytum," he said, laughing as he reached over to me.

"I'm not jealous," I said quickly, blinking at him trying to look away.

"Yes, you are." He squirted a little bit of whipped cream onto my lips and licked it off with his tongue. "I never wanted to lick whipped cream off her pussy," he said, his eyes darkening as he looked me over.

I blush slightly. "So then what are you waiting for?" I said, licking my lips slowly.

He growled, and before I knew what was happening, his lips were on mine, and we were kissing. My hands were on his back, and his hands were pulling my clothes off. I reached and pulled his shirt up, and he tossed it down on the floor. Before I knew what was happening, my bra was off and my shorts were off, and my panties were off, and he was completely naked as well.

He reached down and kissed my nipple and sucked on it gently. "You are just so beautiful, Taytum." He moaned, then licked down the valley between my breasts toward my belly button. And I closed my eyes as I gripped the sheets. I ran my fingers through his hair and tugged on his tresses, and he looked up at me with a little grin.

"You sure do like to play with my hair," he said.

"I do. It's so soft and silky and... well, I love it."

"I'm glad," he said. Then he kissed all the way down between my legs, and I gasped as he grabbed the whipped cream and sprayed a dollop right on my clit. His tongue dove in, and he lapped it up, and I cried out in pleasure as his tongue kept flicking against me.

I bit down on my lower lip as he slipped his tongue inside me, and I knew it wouldn't be long before I had my first orgasm of the evening. It was crazy to me how Noah's touch felt like silk and magic against my body. When I had been with Donovan, he'd been a fumbling fool, and it was like he knew exactly where *not* to touch. I hadn't even been close to an orgasm with him. When I had been with him, I'd try to close my eyes and picture something or someone else, but it had never worked. But with

Noah, with Noah, everything felt amazing. I felt my body shaking as it erupted with its first orgasm, and Noah grunted in satisfaction as he licked me dry. Then he kissed back up my body like I was a tasty treat. His lips pressed against mine, and I could taste the residue of whipped cream on his lips. I kissed him back passionately before grabbing the can from him.

"My turn," I said, winking at him as I sprayed it onto his chest and licked around his nipples.

He groaned as I then sprayed it down his abdomen and licked a trail toward his cock. He looked up at me with hooded eyes, and I licked my lips slowly before spraying it on his manhood. My lips got to work quickly, and I could hear him groaning as my fingers went to the base of his shaft and moved up and down as my lips sucked on the tip of his cock.

"Fuck," he said, "that feels so good." I bobbed my head up and down, loving how hard he felt in my mouth as he kept growing harder and harder.

I shifted forward and got on top of him so he was positioned between my legs. His eyes opened, and I grinned down at him. He reached up and grabbed my breasts and played with my nipples, and I moved forward gently so that I could rub my clit on his shaft. He groaned as he grabbed my hips and moved me again, and I felt the tip of his cock entering me. I shifted slightly, then lifted my hips up and moved down slowly.

"Oh yes," he said as I started bouncing up and down on him.

I closed my eyes as I tilted my head back. I had never felt so in control of a situation. I had never loved being in a position of power like this before. Normally, I was used to missionary. I hadn't thought I'd really enjoy being on top so much, but I loved it. I loved the way he grunted and groaned as I bounced up and down on his cock, and I loved the way he felt inside me. He pinched my nipples, and I fell forward slightly, kissing him on the lips as his hands reached up and played with my hair.

"Don't stop," he said as he grabbed my waist and moved me up and down a little bit faster. I could feel that I was about to come again. And he just grinned as my lower lip trembled. "Fuck yeah," he said. "Don't stop. Don't stop."

I bounced faster and faster, my body feeling hotter and more sensitive than it ever had before. I felt his body stilling underneath me, and all of a sudden, he was coming hard and fast inside me. I screamed as I felt my orgasm hit, and I bounced a couple more times before collapsing on top of him and kissing him on the lips.

"Fuck, that was amazing," he said as he traced a

line down my back. "Fuck. You're just the best, Taytum."

"I know," I said sweetly as I stroked his chest idly. "That was hot," I said. "So hot."

"You're telling me," he groaned. "I don't think I've ever experienced anything like this before."

"Are you just saying that?" I yawned.

"No, I would never just say that. You're going to stay the night, right?" he whispered in my ear as he stroked my back.

"Yeah. I'll probably have to get up early because I'm sure the kids will wake me up, but I'm sure I'll wake up naturally."

"Okay," he said and kissed my forehead. "It's crazy to think that this time last week, I didn't even know you, and now I can't even imagine you not being in my life."

"I know, right?" I said softly. "I can't imagine you not being in my life either. It's funny how things work."

"I know," he said. "It was like we were meant to meet."

"I think so too. You're my Christmas surprise," I said grinning at him.

"You're my Christmas angel," he said. "You know, I've met so many women in my life, and I find them to be so untrustworthy. But you, you're someone special. You're someone I feel I could share my deepest darkest secrets with, and you wouldn't tell a soul, and you wouldn't judge me."

"You can tell me anything, Noah. I know we don't know each other super well, but what we have is really special. And I just want you to know that this is real. All of this is real. What I feel for you is real. This feeling between us, it's—"

"I know," he said as he gave me a kiss on the lips. "This is magical. This is what dreams and perfect Christmas movies are made of."

I laughed then. "You're right of course. It does feel like a Christmas movie."

"Nothing can come between us now," he said. I stared at him. "But you know what?"

"What?" he asked, yawning as well. "It's even better than a Christmas movie."

"Oh yeah? Why is that?"

"Because in Christmas movies, something always happens to make the couple doubt each other, but we don't have to worry about that. We're just in a perfect cocoon, and I can't see anything changing that."

Chapter 32

A BANGING ON THE DOOR MADE ME WAKE UP IN shock. I looked over, and I saw Noah in bed beside me, snoring slightly. I looked at my watch. "Shit!" I hadn't woken up on my own, like I assumed I was going to. And now I wondered if it was the kids here, wondering if Noah had seen where I was?

I quickly shook his shoulder to wake him up. "Morning, sleepyhead," he said, leaning up to give me a kiss as someone banged on the door again.

"I forgot to go to my own room," I said, blinking. "Oh man, what if it's Sammy or Theo or Pollyanna?"

"It's fine," he said, frowning. "I'll get the door."

"Where should I hide?" If I was thinking straight, I would have gone through our adjoining bathroom, but my mind had gone completely blank.

He sighed. "You're not going to hide anywhere, Taytum. I'll see who it is."

"But the kids can't see me in here." I was panicking now.

"Taytum, this is ridiculous. We can't just keep sneaking around. I think we should tell everyone that we're—." He paused and looked at me for a few seconds and smiled softly. "Well, seeing each other." I groaned as he chuckled.

"Really, Noah? Can't we just keep it a secret for a little bit longer?"

"Ridiculous! If we want to spend time together and really get to know each other, people are going to wonder what's going on."

"I guess."

"Hold on," he said. He got out of bed as someone knocked again and pulled on his boxers. "Let me see who it is. Hold on, I'm coming," he shouted as he headed toward the door. He looked back at me and smiled. "Don't worry, Taytum, it will be okay."

"Okay," I said as I lay back in the bed, hoping it wasn't Pop Pop. I really didn't want his parents to think I was some sort of ho.

Noah opened the door and then burst out laughing. "Ethan, man! What's going on? It's early."

"Hey, bro. I wanted to see if you wanted to play a game of golf this morning."

"Well, not right now. I thought you weren't getting back till this evening."

"Yeah, well, I figured I did what I had to do, so I'm here."

I frowned as I just sat there. Why did the voice sound so familiar? I knew I'd heard it before, but I couldn't quite place it.

"So what's going on with you, bro? You want to grab some breakfast or—"

"Well, I mean, I would, but I have some company right now," Noah said, chuckling.

"Company as in?" The voice sounded surprised. "Wait, what?"

"Yeah, Ethan, I mean, I suppose you might as well meet her now."

Noah opened the door wider.

"Taytum, I want you to meet my brother Ethan. Ethan, this is Taytum."

The fates were playing the cruelest joke on me because the worst thing in the world happened. Ethan St. James walked into the bedroom, and my jaw dropped.

"You!" I said, pointing at him.

He raised an eyebrow, looked at his brother, and then looked back at me.

"It is me, indeed." He nodded.

He looked thoughtful for a couple of seconds. "And just who is Taytum to you, Noah?"

"Fuck," I whispered under my breath. "I'm dead meat."

"Taytum is the nanny." Noah chuckled. "I know, I know. How did I start dating the nanny when she's only been here a couple of days, but we just hit it off."

"Taytum is the nanny?" Ethan raised an eyebrow. "Whose nanny?"

"Pollyanna, Sammy, and Theo's, of course." Noah shook his head, frowning.

"What are you talking about?" Ethan frowned now. "She's the Christmas nanny that Lulu hired months ago? I thought her name was Annie."

"Yeah, that's Taytum's real name, but she goes by Taytum because it's her middle name. She's Annie Taytum."

"Really?" Ethan folded his arms and shook his head. "So do you want to tell him, or shall I tell him?" Ethan said, and I bit down on my lower lip.

Noah frowned. "What's going on here? Tell me what?"

"Ethan and I met on the train." I sighed. "We were actually sitting in the same carriage."

"Oh," Noah said, frowning. "I didn't know that. Why didn't you tell me?"

"I didn't know that he was your brother."

"Yeah, you didn't know that I was Ethan St.

James, maybe because you'd never even heard of our family before that moment."

I bit down on my lower lip, and Noah frowned.

"What's going on? What are you talking about, Ethan?"

"So Taytum here was on the train, surprising her boyfriend at the time with a magic trick or pretending she was going to do some magic trick."

I could feel my face going red. The story sounded absolutely ridiculous. And what was worse was that it was true.

"What magic trick?" Noah asked, blinking. "What the hell is going on here?"

"Taytum here was on the train because she wanted to surprise her boyfriend who was going home for Christmas because she thought he would propose to her and be excited. Well, it turns out her boyfriend wasn't so excited and had another girl. And Taytum here was not happy about it, which I know because she called her friend on the phone and complained."

I looked at Noah, whose face was turning suspicious.

"Taytum, is this true?"

I nodded slowly as I glared at Ethan. What a jerk. Couldn't he have taken me to the side and asked me what was going on instead of just blurting out the truth like this?

"So I don't know what her game is here, bro, but she obviously has some sort of plan because she's not Annie and she's not a nanny. And the fact that she was hoping her boyfriend was going to propose two days ago, and now she's in bed with you, leads me to believe that she's got some heck of a new plan going."

"It's not like that, Noah, please. I—"

"So you're not Annie? You're not the nanny?"

"No, but—"

"So you've been lying to me this whole time."

"It's not like that, Noah. This is real. I just..."

"I can't," he said, and he stormed out of the bedroom.

Ethan walked over to me and frowned. "I don't know what your game is, young lady, but you're not going to mess around with my family, you hear?"

"You don't even know what's going on. I didn't pretend to be Annie so I could get with your brother. I didn't even know he was rich. It just happened because I saw Donovan, and I didn't want him to think I was a loser that had only gone on the train to surprise him. I…" I burst into tears. "You just ruined it. I really like Noah. Like I really, really like him. I thought he was the one. I thought this was actually going to be my Hallmark Christmas movie moment."

I stopped as Ethan shook his head and sighed.

"Look, lady, I don't know what planet you live on, but life isn't the movies, and life sure isn't a Hallmark Christmas movie, no matter what that is. I don't know why you pretended to be Annie, and I don't know what happened to the real Annie, but I'm telling you this; I think you need to get a grip and a life and figure it out because you're now messing with real people and people who are important to me."

"Noah's important to me too."

"There you are, Nanny Taytum." Pollyanna ran into the room. "It's time for breakfast. You promised pancakes this morning."

"Okay, " I said, nodding and looking at Ethan. "I'll be there in a second, okay?"

"Okay, I'll wait in the kitchen."

I looked at Ethan and sighed. "Do you want me to pack up my stuff now or…?"

"Go and make them breakfast, Taytum, then all of us will have a discussion afterward." He glared at me. "While you pack your bags because you're out of here."

Chapter 33

Tears streamed down my face, and as I returned to my room to quickly put on some clothes, it suddenly struck me that I hadn't cried when I'd found out about Donovan. I mean, I cried because I was in shock, but I hadn't cried because I was in pain. I hadn't cried because it had ended. I'd cried because he'd been cheating on me, and I was embarrassed and humiliated, but I hadn't cried because my heart was broken. Yet here I was feeling like the world had just ended because Noah had found out I was lying.

I hated Ethan St. James, but more than that, I hated myself. I should have told Noah right away. I should have admitted the truth and let him decide whether he wanted to get to know me better. But I'd taken that away from him, and I'd let him believe that I was this honest young nanny who wanted nothing from him but just to have an enjoyable evening, which was true in some ways. I didn't want his money or status that might come from dating him. I just liked his company. I liked talking to him. I liked sparring with him. I felt a connection to him. But I knew it would be hard for him to believe that now.

I started packing my things. Even though Pollyanna had gone to the kitchen and was waiting for me to make pancakes. I had a feeling Noah was telling Lulu and Nana J and Pop Pop the truth about me. I had a feeling they were all about to find out I was a fraud, and I was slightly nervous that they'd come rushing to my room and tell me to pack my bags and get out now.

I quickly called Danielle as I packed up my case.

"Hey, girl! So I'm just going to the train station to figure out the tickets."

"Don't bother," I said softly, sobbing.

"Oh no! What's happened? Shit, don't tell me the real Annie showed up?"

"No," I said, gulping and swallowing hard. "I messed up," I whined.

"Oh no! Taytum, what's wrong? What happened?"

"Do you remember I told you about the man on the train?"

"Hmm, the rude one?" she asked quickly.

"Yeah. Well, guess what?"

"What?"

"He's Noah's brother Ethan, and he told Noah everything."

"Oh shit! So he told Noah that you're certifiably mad?"

"Thanks very much, thanks for nothing, Danielle, that's not funny."

"I'm sorry, but I'm guessing he told Noah that you were on the train hoping that your boyfriend would propose and instead you got dumped."

"That's not exactly how it happened, Danielle."

"I know. I know. So are you coming home then? Do you want me to wait for you at the train station?"

"I'm packing my stuff now. I'm not sure what I'm going to do. I want to speak to Noah before I leave. I want to explain everything to him so he knows that."

"Mommy!"

"Taytum?"

Sammy came running into my room, and I looked up and blinked.

"Hey Sammy, what's going on?"

"Nanny Taytum, I'm hungry. Pollyanna said you're making pancakes, and we've been waiting for ten minutes, and you still haven't come."

"Oh!" I said, blinking at the little boy. "Isn't Nana J there?"

"No."

"What about Pop Pop or your Uncle Noah?"

"No one's in the kitchen but us."

"Not even your Uncle Ethan?"

"I didn't even know Uncle Ethan was back home yet. Are you coming?" He headed over to me and tugged on my shirtsleeve.

"Please, I'm hungry, and I want to go to the park again."

Danielle laughed in my ear. "Well, it seems like you're still the nanny for the time being."

"I don't know what's going on. Noah stormed out of the room, and I felt like he was definitely going to tell everyone, and I'd be told to leave." I bit down on my lower lip. "Why hasn't he told anyone yet?"

"I don't know, but girl, I'm going to get the first ticket I can. I'm going to come up there."

"No, don't bother. I'm just going to be coming back down soon anyway."

"Then we'll come back down together. You need support."

"Are you sure, Danielle?"

"I'm sure!"

"But what about Isabella?"

236

"We'll tell her everything when we get back."

"Okay, thank you. I love you."

"I love you too, girl. Now, go make the kids some pancakes, and I'll let you know when I'm going to arrive. Just send me the address, and I'll catch a cab."

"Sounds good," I said and then hung up.

"Okay, Sammy, you want to go and make those pancakes now?"

"Yes, please, Nanny Taytum. You know what?"

"What?" I said as we made our way to the kitchen.

"You're my most favorite nanny ever."

"Really?" I stared at him in surprise and pleasure.

"Yeah, you're not bossy and mean like some of them. Sometimes they shout at us, and I don't like that." His little lip quivered.

"Oh, honey, I'm sorry. No one should be shouting at you."

"I know. It makes me sad when they shout."

We got into the kitchen, and I was just about to ask him something else when he ran away from me.

"She's here. She's going to make pancakes now."

"Where have you been?" Pollyanna said, staring at the clock on the wall. "We're absolutely starving."

I looked at her and just smiled. "Well, I'm here now. Let's make these pancakes."

I went to the cupboard and looked for some flour and told Pollyanna to get some eggs from the fridge. And I told Theo to look for a mixing bowl. I was just about to pull up a recipe on my phone when I heard footsteps in the doorway. I turned to look, and it was Noah. He was frowning as he surveyed the scene.

"We need to talk," he said curtly.

I nodded. "Sure!"

"Do you have to talk right now, Uncle Noah? Nanny Taytum is making pancakes."

"Can you guys not have cereal?" he said, frowning. "I need to talk to Nanny Taytum right now, and it can't wait."

"But—" Sammy started and pressed his lips together as Noah gave him a look.

"I'll get the bowls," Pollyanna said in a resigned tone.

"Thank you," I said softly. Then headed over to Noah.

"Let's go to the library," he said. "I don't want to talk in here."

"Okay, " I said and nodded. "I'm so sorry I—"

"Enough!" he snapped. "We'll talk in the library."

He walked ahead of me, and I let out a deep sigh. I had a feeling this was not going to go well. Noah had never spoken to me like that before. I mean, he'd teased me, and he'd been grumpy, but he'd never been mean and snappy. He was mad, and

I understood why, but I just didn't know how to fix it. I didn't know what I could do or say to let him know that what we had was real. But I wouldn't be surprised if he didn't believe anything I had to say now. I wouldn't believe me either.

Chapter 34

"Noah, before you say anything, please let me—"

"I'm not letting you spew more lies." Noah slammed the door behind me as we entered the library. His eyes were spitting daggers at me, and I felt them piercing my heart.

"Can I just explain?" I stared at his face and wondered if I should try to tell a joke to lighten the mood. "I know an old lady that—" The glare he gave me told me this was not the right time.

"So Taytum, whose real name I assume is not Annie Taytum?"

"Um...no, but..." My voice trailed off, and I just shook my head. "There is no Annie in my name."

"And how many years of nannying experience do you have?"

"Um, a couple of days..." I swallowed hard as he folded his arms.

"A couple of days?" He shook his head. "Not including your time here?"

"Including my time here."

"And your degree?"

"It's in art and design. I'm an illustrator. That part was true. I used to illustrate other people's books, but I lost my job, so now I'm hoping to write my own book and illustrate it."

"Why did you pretend you were Annie?"

"Because Donovan, my ex, was behind me..." I sighed. "And I was embarrassed and humiliated, and I didn't really intend to lie...I was going to jump out of the limo when we went a couple of blocks, but then you were so rude, and I wanted to put you in your place, and you mentioned the pay...well, it was enticing."

"So it was all about the money after all?"

"No. I mean, yes in a way. At first. The amount did shock me, and it did make me think I could take the job. But after talking, I knew I wanted to be around you. You made me laugh. You turned me on. That first night we talked all night about ourselves, and I've never felt more connected to anyone before in my life..." I reached out and touched his arm. "Please, Noah, you have to understand...I didn't want to keep the lie up, but I just didn't know how to come clean without you hating me. A bit like you do now."

"I don't hate you, Taytum." He sighed. "I'm not happy with you, but I don't hate you."

"Yes, you do. You want me to pack up my bags and leave. I can see it in your eyes." I looked away from him as I could feel tears about to fall.

"No, Taytum, I don't. In fact, I have something for you." He pursed his lips. "I am so mad at you right now. You don't even know."

"I do know actually." I looked pleadingly into his eyes. "There are four words I want to say, but I'm not sure you want to hear them right now."

"Really?" He cocked his head to the side.

"What?"

"Do you really think I want to have sex right now?"

"Huh?" I looked around the room. "Am I being punked? What are you talking about?"

"Put it in now." He raised his eyebrows at me.

"WHAT?" I almost shouted.

"Those are the four words you wanted to tell me, right?"

"No. Are you out of your mind?" For a moment, I thought he was going to start laughing, but the moment passed, and his face was serious.

"So what were you going to say then?"

"I was going to say, I think I'm falling." I lowered

my voice and looked down at the ground in embarrassment.

"You think what?" He took a step closer to me.

"I think I'm falling," I mumbled again.

"Falling where? To the ground? Off a cliff?" His voice held humor in it and I looked up at him.

"Falling for you." I glared at him.

"Is that so?" His eyes bore into mine, and I nodded. "Is Taytum falling, or is Annie?" I winced at his comment.

"I suppose I deserve that." I sighed and headed toward the door. "I should pack my stuff and go."

"Wait," he said, though he didn't move to stop me. I looked back at him with a raised eyebrow.

"Yes?"

"I got this for you." He reached into his pocket and pulled out some white tissue paper. "I was going to wrap it and give it to you for Christmas, but..."

"What is it?"

"Open it and see." He shrugged as he handed it to me. I took it from him gingerly, my heart racing. I pulled the tissue away and gasped when I saw the gold locket in my hands.

"What is this?" I blinked as I gazed up at him, but he didn't say anything. I opened it, and my heart thudded as I saw two photos in the locket. One of him and one of me. I turned it over and saw an inscription that made me want to cry. The inscription read *This moment is about us.* "Noah?"

"You said you had this dream that your soul mate would give you a locket." He shrugged. "I thought it would be romantic."

"But wait, what?" I blinked at him. "When did you get this?"

"Yesterday." He made a face. "I guess I'm a fool."

"Why did you get this?"

"Because I knew..." He shrugged. "I don't think I'm falling, Taytum. I've already fallen."

"And now you want to take it all back?"

"No..." he said with a small smile. "I'm not giving you up."

"But, but you're so mad at me. You..."

"I'm mad that you didn't tell me the truth." He shrugged. "I had a feeling you weren't Annie, though. You just didn't seem like you knew what you were doing with the kids. You treat them well, but you certainly didn't act like a Super Nanny."

"What gave me away?"

"The kids walked all over you." He laughed. "You didn't seem to know how to control them, and you seemed too nervous about having to be with them all day."

"I guess I'm not as good of an actress as I thought."

"Don't lie to me again, Taytum. There's nothing you can't tell me, okay?"

I nodded. "So you forgive me?"

"I forgive you." He leaned forward and kissed me. "I don't want you to leave. Say you'll stay."

"Of course, as long as everyone else is okay with it."

"Everyone is fine with it." He beamed and touched the side of my face. There was a hesitant look on his face. "Except for maybe Ethan, but he'll come around."

"He hates me." I sighed.

"He just doesn't understand how we could have fallen for each other so quickly, but then he's never been in love before." He brushed some hair away from my face. "I know this sounds crazy, but I knew from the first moment I saw you, Taytum, I love you."

"I love you too, Noah St. James." I kissed him tenderly. "You're even better than a Hallmark leading man."

"I should hope so." He laughed. "I'm real."

"Oh yes, you are so very real." I melted against him as he wrapped his arms around my waist, and I felt his hardness against me. I reached up and grabbed his face and kissed him passionately. "Thank you for the locket. It means the world to me."

"Thank you for being the woman who makes me laugh and dream." He ran his fingers down my back. "I can't wait to make a lifetime of memories with you."

"Me too." I grinned at him. "Oh and by the way, Danielle is on the way to Little Kimble. She can still stay, right?"

"Of course, your friends are my friends. I can't wait to meet her. In fact, I'm sure the entire family can't wait."

"Aside from Ethan, though." I giggled. "I'm sure he'll want her gone as well."

"Probably," Noah said as his hands pulled up my top. "But let's not talk about my annoying brother right now. I have other things I'd like to do."

"Ooh, Mr. St. James, whatever are you talking about?" I giggled as I pulled his top up as well, and I couldn't stop myself from thinking just how lucky I was. This really was going to be the best Christmas ever.

Thank you for reading Eggnog, Mistletoe, & Noah St. James. The next book in the series is Cocoa, Ivy, & Ethan St. James and features Ethan St. James and Danielle. You can get it here. Read an exclusive excerpt from the book below.

Join my mailing list to never miss any of my books here.

.   .   .

*C*ocoa, Ivy, & Ethan St. James Excerpt
       Blurb

*E*than St. James is the Scrooge of my Life...
       Most people have heard of love at first sight, but what I experienced with Ethan St. James was the exact opposite. He's the brother of my best friend Taytum's boyfriend and an absolute horror. I can't believe I have to spend the holiday season with him.

The problem is he thinks my best friend is an opportunist who is using his brother because he's rich. And now, due to a misunderstanding, he thinks I'm trying to snag his other brother. Like, I need to trap someone into a relationship with me. There's no planet in the galaxy where I would feel desperate enough to date a St. James.

But when Ethan approaches me with an offer to stop my best friend from leaving and traveling across the world, I stop and listen. He wants us to pretend to get engaged to show his brother and Taytum that they are moving too fast. I don't think it's the best plan ever, but I'm not ready to lose her from my life. Especially considering she hasn't had the best taste in men in the past.

So now, here we are. Pretending we've fallen in

love at first sight. I'm not sure we're convincing anyone, but the Christmas season seems to make everyone believe in romance.

hapter One
Three children dressed in bright thick wool coats stood on the street in front of me singing Silent Night. Their voices were quite beautiful as they sang their hearts out on the cold street. I reached into my wallet and pulled $5 out of my purse and dropped it into their bucket.

"Thank you, ma'am."

"Thank you. Have a Merry Christmas." I nodded at the girl that had spoken. The other two continued singing, and I soon realized that the main girl had been the harmony in the group.

"You too," the girl with the snowman headband beamed and then started singing again.

"Happy Hanukkah," the girl next to her said.

"Happy Kwanzaa," the one next to her said. And we all laughed. It really was the holiday season, my favorite time of the year.

"Merry Christmas. Happy Hanukkah and happy Kwanzaa to you, too." I continued on my way to Penn Station. I loved living in New York City. I loved being around so many diverse cultures and having the opportunity to try so many different restaurants full of delicious foods. I could have Ethiopian one night and Chinese another; Mexican on the weekend, and if I was just feeling absolutely homesick, I'd grab a slice of Chicago style pizza.

"I hope Little Kimble has some good food." I mumbled to myself before pulling my phone out of my handbag. I checked my phone screen as I made my way into the train station, I had no more text messages from my best friend Taytum, and I was worried about her. Taytum had gone to little Kimble, hoping to surprise her boyfriend, Donovan. She thought that he'd be exhilarated and excited that she wanted to join him and his family for Christmas. Unfortunately, it hadn't worked out that way. He'd been cheating on her and to her surprise the journey ended up with her being dumped. It hadn't surprised me, though. I'd known he was a jackass from the very first moment I met him, and he'd asked if I'd wanted to go to the bathroom and suck him off for $100. I'd tried to tell Taytum, but she thought he was joking and testing me as a friend. She was naive like that. She always wanted to see the best in everyone, especially men that she dated. Unfortunately for her, every last guy she dated was an asshole.

However, even though Taytum had bad taste in men, she never listened when I told her I could tell right away that she was dating an asshole because she just wanted to be in love. I still loved her and would always support her, but I didn't want her to have another bad relationship. That was why I was now on my way to little Kimble to save her from a potentially horrific new relationship. When she got dumped by Donovan, she'd pretended to be a girl called Annie. And took a nanny position for a rich family called the St James's. Everything had gone swimmingly the first couple of days until one of the brothers arrived and had blown her cover. He'd recognized her from the train and knew she wasn't Annie. She'd fallen out with Noah, the eldest brother, but now supposedly he'd forgiven her and they were in love, but I wasn't sure what to think about the situation. It all seemed way too fast for me. So I'd decided to go to Little Kimble to check on everything myself. I'd even taken off work; even though my job didn't know that yet.

I pulled out my phone and quickly got my work number. It rang a couple of times and then the receptionist Candace answered the phone.

"Thank you for calling Clean Harbors Accounting services. How may I help you? This is Candace speaking."

"Hey, Candace, it's me, Danielle."

"Hey, Electra," she said, giggling.

"I'm not going by Electra anymore. It didn't quite fit me."

"I was wondering why you said Danielle again,"

she said in an absentminded voice. "What's going on? How come I haven't seen you this morning?"

"I'm at the train station."

"Oh? Going somewhere?"

"Yeah. I'm headed to Little Kimble in Connecticut."

"Connecticut?" She sounded surprised. "Why are you going to Connecticut?"

"Do you remember my best friend, Taytum?"

"Yeah. She's the girl with the long, dark hair, right?"

"Yeah, well, she's kind of got a job there now, and I'm not sure it's working out, and she might kind of need me to rescue her." I knew I sounded vague, but I didn't really want to get into the entire story with her.

"Oh gee," Candace sounded worried. "I hope she's okay."

"Me, too. Well, anyway, I was just calling to say I'm not going to work for the rest of the week."

"Oh, okay. What do you want me to tell the boss?"

"Can you just say an emergency came up?"

"Sure thing. Will you be back next week?"

"I don't know. Depends on if Taytum is okay and if I need to take her on a de-stressing trip. Her boyfriend dumped her and she just lost her job. And well, you know how it goes."

"You're such a good friend, Danielle." I could hear the sounds of clacking as she typed something.

"Oh, thanks, Candace, but I should go now. I want to try and catch the next train, and I think I only have 15 minutes to get the ticket and get to the platform."

"Okay, sounds good. Tell Taytum, the way to get over one man is to get under another one."

I started laughing at her comment. "I think that might be the problem." I hung up quickly before she could ask me what I meant and made my way to the ticket kiosks so that I could get a ticket to Little Kimble. I was excited to see these St. James brothers. The way she talked, they were the younger and better looking Baldwin brothers of Connecticut. Super-hot and super rich. And even if I was only there for one night, I needed to see some eye candy and possibly get my flirt on. I also wanted to make sure Noah wasn't another Donovan.

I needed to see the guy that had convinced my best friend to sleep with him the first night that she met him. Because Taytum just wasn't that sort of girl. I mean, I told her plenty of times that she should just loosen up and have fun. But she was so caught up in romance movies and romance books and had a plan and a timeline for everything, that it had never happened before. I wanted to meet the man that had gotten into her panties on the first night. I hoped he had been worth it.

The ticket popped out of the machine and I put my credit card back into my purse and looked for the sign to show me which platform to go to. My phone started ringing then and I saw it was Taytum. I answered quickly so I could let her know I was on the way.

"Hey, how's it going?" I was excited to see her.

"I'm okay," she said softly, whispering into the phone.

"Oh, no. What happened?" I frowned as I looked around for a coffee shop. I needed some caffeine. Preferably a peppermint mocha or a gingerbread latte, with a scone or chocolate croissant.

"Oh not much. I spoke to Noah about everything and I just—."

"You just what?" My heart was pounding. "Do you want to come home?"

"No, not at all. I told you he's going to give me another chance, right? He said I can-"

"Wait. What? *He's* going to give you another chance. More like he's happy you're still going o have sex with him."

"No, silly," she giggled.

"I mean, we will most probably have sex again because I'm falling for him and he's falling for me and-"

"Wait, what?!" What is going on, Taytum?"

"We had a really long, in-depth conversation, and I explained to him everything and he said he's willing to give me another chance and they're willing to see how I go as a nanny. And I said, I wouldn't expect the same pay that he was offering initially because I was accepting it under false pretenses-"

"Oh, my God. Taytum. So you're staying?"

"Yeah. I like him. I really, really like him. And I know this is really fast, and I know things with Donovan just ended."

"Oh, girl, I don't care about Donovan. He was a douche bag."

"Why didn't you tell me you thought that, Danielle? I wouldn't have-" She paused and then giggled. "Okay. Maybe I would have continued seeing him, but it would have made me pause."

"Yeah, right. You know how many guys you've dated that I've told you are bad news and you've still continued to date them."

"I know," she sighed. "But, yeah, I just wanted to update you. Everything's okay now and-"

"Hold on a second, Taytum. There's something I need to tell you."

"What is it? I'm on my way to Little Kimble."

"You what?!" She screeched. "Really?"

"Yeah. I need to make sure everything's going well with my own two eyes. Okay?"

"Of course. I already told Noah you were still coming, but I wasn't sure if you were really going to make it or not."

"So there is one thing I should say before you get here." Taytum's voice sounded a little bit hesitant and I frowned.

"What is it? Tell me."

"So.... Ethan St James."

"That's Noah's brother."

"Yeah, his second oldest brother."

"Okay. What about him?"

"He might not be so happy about you arriving."

You can get it here.

Printed in Great Britain
by Amazon